THE Power OF THE V

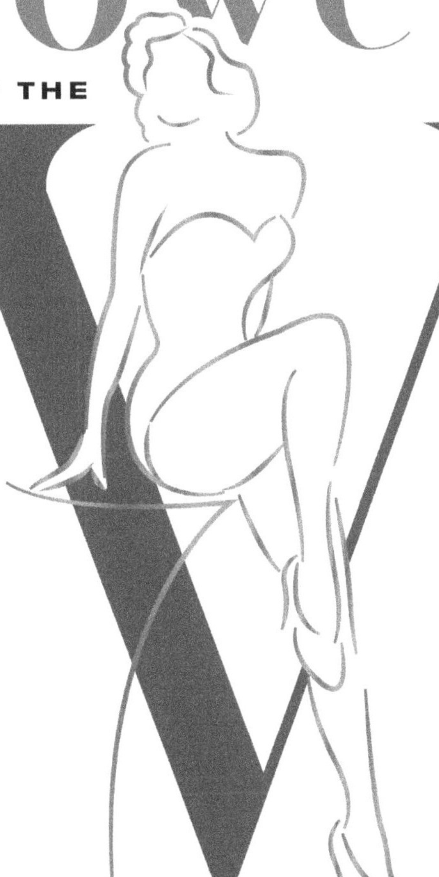

VISIONARY AUTHOR

COURAGEOUS STORIES OF VULNERABILITY

FOREWORD BY Felicia S. Barwell

THE Power

OF THE

VISIONARY AUTHOR

Debbie LeSean

The Power of the V

Manuscript editing
Catherine LaCroix

Book Creation and Design
Ellese & Co Creative
www.elleseandco.com

ISBN: 978-1-7367808-5-5

Printed in the United States of America

Foreword

It is my distinct honor to invite you to journey with seven courageous women as they unveil their personal vulnerabilities. Removing masks that have literally held them hostage, shackled and captive. Masks that suffocated them mind, body, and soul, leaving them to feel helpless, hopeless, and powerless. Seven women obscuring the beauty of their wonderful creation and creativity behind hardened masks.

As you travel with these Sisters, sharing in their pain and sensing the emotions that birthed these pages, don't be alarmed if you find your eyes welling up with their very own cleansing tears. Each one is precious — a reminder on the page of this shared journey. Let the sentiment of this powerful and liberating anthology flow.

Reprieve for a moment as these beautiful souls did before they removed their masks to codify these transformative revelations to forever remember the power within. Don't stop your journey until you have harnessed the power of your vulnerabilities. Wait for the moment to exhale and celebrate.

I am honored to have been part of this anthology and privileged to have seen the birth of newness of life reigning from **The Power of the V.**

"And we all, with unveiled face, continually seeing as in a mirror the glory of the Lord, are progressively being transformed into His image from [one degree of] glory to [even more] glory, which comes from the Lord, [who is] the Spirit."
~ 2 Corinthians 3:18 (AMP)

Reverend
Felicia S. Barwell, MDiv

Virginia Union University
Samuel Dewitt Proctor School of Theology

Follow Rev. Felicia S. Barwell on [f] Felicia.Lambbarwell

A NOTE FROM THE

Visionary

Debbie LeSean

Debbie LeSean is THE Coach to call when you're ready to turn turmoil into triumph. Debbie is focused on helping women embrace the rain, celebrate the rainbow then be the sun in another woman's storm by sharing their story. Her God-given assignment is to help women heal their heart and master their emotions with the use of a pen. Her job is to reframe limiting beliefs, eliminate doubt, and provide customized techniques on inking their way to victory.

Debbie holds a B.S. from VCU & an M.A. in Counseling from Liberty University. She credits the streets of New York with teaching her life skills that a classroom could not.

Follow her on (O)coachdebbielesean (f) debbielesean
or check out her website at www.**debbielesean**.com

Vulnerability. Courage. Mask Off. Authenticity. Transparency.

Those were the things required of these seven women in signing up to co-author this book. I kept feeling in my spirit that it was time for women to shed light about those things we secretly cry about in the dark. I put the call out there for authors, not knowing if anyone would show up, but they did. They said, "Debbie, I've been holding this inside for too long." I provided the safe space, the coaching and the guidance needed to MOVE these women along in this journey called life.

Each of them carrying a sacred story inside that very few people knew about. Each of them transitioning from one phase to the next in life. Everyday women, like me and you. At some point in life, you may experience something that you hold dear to your heart. Maybe at some point, you will possess the boldness and confidence needed to step on the head of Fear, Judgement and Uncertainty like these seven women, and tell your story. When or if that time comes, I'll be waiting to help you *Tell Your Story*.

Seven women: Ashley, Angela H., Angela J., Lititca, Millicent, Shana, Sonya. Different backgrounds, different stories, different walks of life. One commonality: **The Power of the V**. One goal: Tell the story! They persevered, together. They cried, together. They journeyed, together. They became published authors, together. This is what happens when Queens unite!

The number seven. Seven is the number of **completeness and perfection** (both physical and spiritual). It derives much of its meaning from being tied directly to God's creation of all things. Isaiah 43:19 — speaks of God doing a NEW thing. He did it for these seven women and he can do it for you!

Sit back and enjoy,

Debbie

TABLE OF
Contents

1

RIPPING OFF THE

Band-Aid

Millicent
Little-Glover

Millicent Little-Glover is new on the writing scene but she'll leave you wanting more. Millicent grew up in a small town in Southeast Georgia where she graduated high school. She attended Troy University where she received both bachelor's and master's degrees in Psychology and Post-Secondary Education respectively.

Millicent's interests go beyond writing, she also enjoys reading, shopping, crafting, and spending time with family and friends. Her love for helping people has fostered a nearly 20-year career in working with adults with developmental disabilities.

She currently resides in coastal Georgia and is married with 3 children. She has four grandsons whom she adores.

When a Band-Aid is ripped off, it leaves a sore vulnerable. Exposing a wound to open air so it can breathe can be a terrible mistake. However, as awful as it sounds, removing a protective layer can actually be a good idea. "A small initial scab will help stop the bleeding, but if left for too long, it will do more harm than good." "You don't want it to mature too much because it increases scarring."

Allow me to rip off my Band-Aid...

I was young and popular. I was a varsity cheerleader. Friday nights meant football and basketball games and the dances to follow. Riding "the strip" with friends was a popular pastime. We'd fill up the gas tank and drive at least 100 miles on any given Friday night. I had everything going for me, or so I thought. I was active in the student council. I was raised in a two-parent home where I was loved and adored by my parents and siblings. Of course, that was not without occasional practical jokes, pranks, and sibling rivalry. However, those good times and memories were all overshadowed by one horrific night. I was raped by an acquaintance. I knew him. He knew me. He knew my family. How could he do this? Why would he? Who knew a night out would lead to the worst night of my life? At age sixteen, my life, as I knew it, was over. The shame... the humiliation... the self-blame crept in while innocence crept out... I was totally humiliated. I felt that anyone could look at me and just know what had happened.

I began to alienate myself from my peers. I no longer wanted to attend sleepovers or football games. I didn't appear to be quite as popular anymore. I felt as if the entire world knew. There was nothing I could do to restore my innocence or to look at myself in the mirror without feeling disgusted. At a time when my friends were getting excited about prom and high school class rings, I was praying that no one would ever find out about the vile violation that had occurred to me. And they didn't. You see... I didn't report the rape. I didn't want to talk about it. I didn't want to think about it. I hoped that if I ignored it, it would go away. Yet, instead, it manifested itself in my adult life as promiscuity, lack of feelings and emotions regarding relationships, and an inability to trust. The promiscuity eventually gave way to sheer disgust with sex and being physically naked with anyone. I, ironically, began to suffer from body dysmorphic disorder (BDD). The remnants remain to this day. The rape took away everything yet also opened the door for everything. As years went by, the memories of it all opened the door for smoking marijuana, drinking, low self-esteem and uncertainty, and failed relationships.

The rape left me emotionally and behaviorally scarred. I pushed people away, friends I had known for years. My behavior changed so much that I began to dress modestly. I still wear a tank top like an undershirt as a security blanket. A rape victim, in some cultures, may be viewed as being *damaged*. I viewed myself this way for many years. And to some extent, I still do.

Recovering from rape varies from survivor to survivor. I recovered by suppressing it. I hid my feelings. I didn't want to discuss or even think about the events of that night. I buried the secret so far down into my soul that no one else knew the truth unless I felt compelled to share it with them. The rape stunted my emotional growth. In every adult opposite-sex relationship I encountered, I thought and acted as my sixteen-year-old self. Not knowing how to love, how to trust, how to be affectionate without it being forced was foreign to me. I was psychologically depressed. I no longer found joy in things that were once important to me. I experienced appetite and weight changes. Sleep difficulties and low energy also emerged in adulthood. Depression loomed like a big black cloud, promising a severe storm. I didn't know at what moment the storm cloud would erupt. But I knew it would. And it did. It erupted in the form of resentment, anger, and self-loathing.

A few years passed. The resentment, anger, and self-loathing remained dormant. Age sixteen was in the rearview mirror, and my college days approached. I learned that I was pregnant four months into my freshman year after a failed relationship. Another chance for me to be a normal young lady escaped my grasp once again. The hopes of college parties, hanging out with my roommate, pledging to a sorority… *gone*. Here I was again, angry, disappointed, and certain that nothing could or would ever go right for me. From age nineteen to forty-nine, I suffered in what I thought was silence. However, my silence was loud. It was deafening. Every encounter with an adult male, outside of family members, was forced. It wasn't sincere. It wasn't love. It was indifferent. It was a test of their aptitude to determine if they loved me enough to put up with the verbal and emotional abuse I inflicted upon them.

Once or twice, when I thought there was a small chance of genuinely loving someone and being in a meaningful relationship, I found myself having to be in control of every relationship to ensure my safety and exert my power. I had to control the money, where we lived, what we did... everything. Otherwise, I felt violated and vulnerable. That wasn't a relationship. That was a dictatorship. I became the aggressor. I became the perpetrator. And little did I know that the Band-Aid was working itself off.

From ages nineteen to forty-six, I dated. I even got married. I wasn't happy. I was constantly depressed. I didn't enjoy anyone's company but my own. I appreciated solitude. I wanted to be alone. I needed to be left alone.

In 2017, I met my now-husband. He and I met at a behavioral conference. How ironic, right? We didn't immediately click, though. We didn't lock eyes across a crowded room. Instead, he asked a question to the presenter, and I knew at that moment that he was smart and safe. Safe in that he wanted to know the best way to handle a person with certain behaviors. If memory serves me correctly, he also inquired about medication management. For years I sought men that I thought could physically protect me against any perpetrator. Yet, I knew this man would be the protector of my heart.

Our first date lasted five hours. I eventually shared my past trauma with him. He didn't run away. He didn't flinch. He simply stated, "You do know that it was no accident that God would allow us to meet, right?" He had dated someone previously that was a victim of rape. While he was no rape crisis counselor or an expert on the subject, I truly believe God fashioned him for me and for a time such as this. Once we were married, he didn't find it odd or even annoying when I'd wake up during the middle of the night because of a nightmare. He never asked, "You still having nightmares after all these years?" He doesn't question that I check obsessively the doors each night, making sure that they're locked… sometimes twice. While I've shared the events of "that night" with him, not once has he considered me damaged goods. That was a label I gave myself and shared with him early on in our courtship. I tried to hide the pain, the shame, the embarrassment. He wouldn't and doesn't allow me to be or feel "victim shamed."

He saw straight through the tough as nails façade. He peered past the "have it all together on the outside but crumbling on the inside" double life I was living. He cared. He truly cared, then and now. However, it was still hard to push past the pain, shame, and self-loathing to love myself totally and completely so that I could fully love him. I questioned my mental health status. I read and studied mental health disorder symptoms and identified with all of them. I was certain I had more than Post Traumatic Stress Disorder (PTSD). Then, I obsessed over the fact that what if I have bipolar disorder? I exhibited the signs of a negative outlook on life, reduced need for sleep, and poor eye contact with others. Borderline personality disorder? I displayed all the classic signs, such as poor self-image, impulsive and self-damaging behaviors, feeling empty, unstable relationships. Social anxiety?What if the rape had taken everything, yet given me those things? I knew I wasn't right and didn't feel right. I knew I wanted to be normal. I knew I wanted to ease the pain that I had bottled up for so very long. I wanted to scream. I wanted to cry. I wanted to be whole. There were times I wanted to die. Wanting to die wasn't a new feeling. I attempted suicide years earlier.

I don't speak much of my suicide attempt as I'm more ashamed of it than the actual rape itself. Ashamed that I survived. Now everyone knows. At least with the rape, no one knew. Some days were so dark I didn't want to get out of bed. I didn't want to go on. I didn't know how to function. Yet, I had to. I was a mother. So, I would muster up the courage and smile to be there, physically, for my baby girl. Having a daughter intensified my lack of trust in men. My daughter had no clue that whenever she was out on a date or out of my sight, my heart sank, and I worried tremendously about her. I didn't want what had happened to me to ever happen to her. So, I became a helicopter mom. I had to know where she was all the time and who she was hanging out with. That drove a wedge between us during her teenage years. I can recall her asking me once after I called to a party she was attending, "Why do you hate me?" It wasn't that I hated her. I hated myself. I hated what I had become. I hated that I thought the worse of people. All people. All the time.

The suicide attempt and surviving rape, to me, were synonymous. It's a feeling of emptiness: a shell of the person I once was. I lived as a shell for many, many years. It wasn't until 2021, thirty-three years later, that I decided to live. I decided to love myself enough to come out of the shell. I shared with my husband that I was tired of hurting and wanted to love him and myself fully, completely. On April 8, 2021, I saw a therapist for the first time. I was sick and tired of being sick and tired. I was so mentally exhausted from carrying the burden of shame and humiliation. I need to give voice to the violation I had suffered. At my first therapy appointment, I shared. I cried. I released. I didn't feel ashamed. Recalling the events of that night made me feel empowered to share, but it also left me completely empty. I poured out my heart and soul regarding the rape for the last time. Or so I thought. I recalled the story, detail by detail, very tearfully. The recount left my soul bare, drained. The session seemed to have lasted forever. Isn't time up yet? How long must I go on? As I shared my story, I can recall the look of gloat and accomplishment on "his" face. How can you feel good about yourself for ruining a person's life?

The second session was easier, much easier. I'm still in therapy. The therapist didn't fix me. Nor did she make me forget the coward that raped me. There's no magic wand to make things right in my world. However, I chose myself. I chose to love myself more than disliking the perpetrator and his actions. I chose to free myself from my past to live in the present and look forward to my future. I allowed myself to be vulnerable enough to share my hurt, pain, and past with someone else. And guess what? *I survived*. The world didn't end because my secret was out. It was actually quite liberating. Being vulnerable doesn't mean being weak. Being vulnerable is the opposite. It means taking risks and exposing yourself to others emotionally. Contrary to popular belief, vulnerability increases our self-worth, allows growth, and helps us overcome negative emotions faster.

Imagine if I had shared my story thirty-three years ago? Imagine if I had been vulnerable and comfortable enough to share my pain all those many years ago? While I can't change the past, I can certainly look to the future with hope and clarity.

To the Person Who Tried to Take My Power

You fractured me. But you didn't break me. I am healed. I am healing. Your cowardly act didn't and doesn't make you a man. A man is like my husband, who loves me despite the psychological damage. You are the exact opposite of a man. You used what you thought was power to control and manipulate a situation that only gave you brief satisfaction. You took away my worth, dignity, and self-respect. You deprived me of my innocence, my intimacy, my power to love, and my confidence. You were manipulative, dishonest, and coercive. I grew up and went through life believing I had no value,feeling unworthy of anyone's affection. I grew up disgusted with myself, ashamed as if I were to blame for your actions. That's how I felt for decades. For decades, I kept a secret that protected you. The guilt, shame, and disgust were so paralyzing that I didn't report the rape, bearing all of this in silence. You've always walked around, free. And seemingly exempt from a guilty conscience. For the rest of your life, I hope you know you assaulted someone. Today, I give you everything you've given me. Everything. I give you everything I didn't deserve and never asked for. The shame, the guilt, lack of self-worth. I return it all. The burden of shame lies with you.

You. Raped. Me.

It has taken me years to say those words to you. The memory floods back from time to time, at the most inopportune times whenever I'm home alone. In a public restroom. Being pulled over during a traffic stop. I'm sure the memories of that night never cross your mind. But for me, that night has been all-consuming. Yet, the reality of it all is that you don't deserve that much credit or energy. While you've escaped the long arm of justice because I didn't report the rape, I wish I had reported it even years later. Even if nothing came of it,you would have experienced a microscopic fraction of the hell I have gone through.

I have transitioned from a bruised caterpillar into a beautiful butterfly who sees and shares hope, love, and light with many. I was once a rape victim. I am now a survivor of rape. You silenced me... until now. I have chosen to release the pain, anger, and hurt so that I can move forward and live, finally. The fractures are being pieced together. My strength is restored. My shame was abandoned.

I am standing in my truth. God's truth. I am fearfully and wonderfully made. I am freed by my own voice and God's own doing. I feel at peace now.

To My Sister Trying to Gain Power

You don't know me, but you are me. You are not alone. Trauma is hard and can rob you of your ability to trust your own feelings. You may feel depressed, guilty, angry, and afraid. It's OK to feel any or all of these things. You didn't deserve any of what happened to you. You don't deserve to be silenced or minimized.

Regardless of your story, you are powerful. You are beautiful, and you will survive. You are surviving. You are not a victim. You are a warrior. Remember while healing that every success, no matter how small, is still progress.

I hear you. I see you. I stand with you. Seek counseling. Find your tribe. Some helpful resources are:

National Sexual Assault Hotline:
1-800-656-HOPE

National Suicide Prevention Hotline:
1-800-273-8255

We deserve so much better than what happened to us. I believe I will be OK. I believe you will, too.

Works Cited

O'Connor, Anahad. "The Claim: Wounds Heal Better When Exposed to Air." *New York Times*, August 1, 2006, www.nytimes.com/2006/08/01/health/01real.html.

Acknowledgements

I cannot express enough thanks to Coach Debbie LeSean for this opportunity and encouragement. Thank you for all the emails, inbox messages, memes, text messages, etc. You inspire me.

To my bestie, Tracy, thank you for always going along with any idea I throw your way. You don't belittle me or make me seem crazy for following my dreams whatever the dream is at the time. #BFFL

To my loving and supportive husband who saw the vision before I could even think of the vision. Your encouragement when times were tough is duly noted and much appreciated. My heartfelt thanks to you. I love you to infinity.

Dedication

I dedicate this chapter to young ladies everywhere especially to my daughters and nieces. I love you. Agape love is the highest form of love. It fosters permanent spiritual growth.

"And now abide faith, hope, love; these three;
but the greatest of these is love."
~ 1 Corinthians 13:13

Reflections

_____

_____

_____

_____

_____

_____

_____

_____

_____

_____

_____

_____

_____

_____

_____

_____

_____

_____

_____

_____

_____

Reflections

_____
_____
_____
_____
_____
_____
_____
_____
_____
_____
_____
_____
_____
_____
_____
_____
_____
_____
_____
_____
_____
_____
_____
_____
_____

Reflections

CHAPTER

II

OBLIVIOUS
Manifestation

Ashley King

Ashley is a Lead Academic Advisor at Reynolds Community College in Richmond, Virginia. A graduate of Norfolk State University, Ashley received a B.A. in Sociology and minored in Criminal Justice. After graduating college, Ashley launched her career at Reynolds where she has been a loyal employee for the past eight years. While working in Higher Education, Ashley actively engaged in many committees, completed a Career Coaching certification through the Virginia Community College System, and served as a mentor for WISE, Women in Search of Excellence. Ashley continues to work as Lead Advisor at Reynolds with plans to pursue a certification in Life Coaching.

Follow Ashley on 📷 @She_her_King
📘 Ash.Renea.7 ▶ Ash Renea

I hold many titles: Wife, Daughter, Sister, Auntie, Cousin, and Friend. However, there's one title I do not hold, and that is Mom. In the beginning, I was OK with this. At a young age, I would always say, "I don't want kids." My mother would tell me to stop saying that before God would grant me my wish. Well, I wasn't worried about that back then. I felt like I had all the time in the world to worry about having children.

At age twelve, I started my menstrual cycle. I remember it like it was yesterday. I thought I was going to die! It was my first time experiencing the excruciating pain of cramps. This was also the start of something I would have to deal with for the rest of my life; this was only the beginning. My menstrual cramps were so terrible that I was already doubled over in pain even on my very first day experiencing my cycle. Little did I know, I would be missing one to two days of school every month due to pain. This cycle continued into my adulthood.

Years passed, and I got used to this cycle of monthly pain. I just kept pushing forward with life and worked through the pain as it came. It was the summer of 2009, and I had just turned twenty-one. I was on summer break from school and working two jobs. I started to experience sharp pains at random hours of the day and night. In the beginning, the pain would wake me up around two in the morning and not subside until about six. No amount of over-the-counter medication would help; I would just be up and in pain.

Now, most people would say, why didn't you go to the ER or see the doctor? Well, because it wasn't happening that frequently at first. I ignored it. I also thought since I was working two jobs and they were both on my feet, maybe this was the issue because my back was hurting pretty bad. I was also a little scared of what the doctor would say. But I couldn't ignore it anymore. This terrible pain started to become more frequent. One day, I was at work, and the pain was so bad it brought me to tears and my knees. This is the day I finally said, "I'm going to the ER."

I went to the ER, but they found nothing. They gave me some meds and sent me on my way. But, deep down, I knew something was wrong. My body just wasn't right, so I went to my primary care doctor. She did all types of tests and took blood samples, but she couldn't figure it out. So, she referred me to an ob-gyn specialist. I set up an appointment with this doctor and ended up having multiple appointments with her. She also found nothing wrong with me. But I knew that I was in pain, and it was only getting worse as the days passed. Eventually, she did an ultrasound. She wanted to see what she could not feel.

After seeing the ultrasound results, we finally got the answers to why I was in so much pain. I had an ovarian cyst the size of, as the doctor described it, "a full-term baby's head." It was sitting right on my left ovary. It had also attached itself to my fallopian tube and was pushing on my back because it was so big, which explained my back pain. I also had another cyst on the opposite ovary. Not as big but big enough that it too needed to be removed. The cyst was so big that my doctor didn't want to waste any more time. She scheduled me for surgery ASAP before the cyst decided to burst and potentially cause more complications.

I was nervous, I was scared, but if that meant no more pain, then I was all in! I had the surgery done and had to stay in the hospital for three days. I had a consultation with my doctor while I was staying in the hospital, and she informed me that I had endometriosis. What is that? Well, I was just as confused and uninformed as you are. I did know that I would live with this condition for the rest of my life and that there is no cure. But I didn't really know, or fully understand, what that meant for me. My doctor gave me a brochure about it and had me watch a video, but that's all. At that time, there wasn't much information on endometriosis. They explained in the brochure and video how it's caused. However, no brochure or video could prepare me for how this would actually change my life moving forward.

What is endometriosis, you ask? It is a disorder in which tissue that normally lines the uterus grows outside the uterus. This means that tissue can be found on the ovaries, fallopian tubes, or intestines. Retrograde menstrual flow is likely the cause of endometriosis. The most common symptoms caused by endometriosis are abdominal pain, infertility, menstrual irregularities, and ovarian cysts. Endometriosis is classified into one of four stages based upon the exact location, extent, and depth of the condition. As well as the presence and severity of scar tissue and the presence and size of the endometrial implants in the ovaries. What stage of endometriosis do you think that I was in? If you guessed stage four, you guessed right.

When I was first diagnosed with endometriosis, I was at stage two. In 2019, I was experiencing some familiar pains. All too familiar, so I went back to my ob-gyn. Because she had already classified me at stage two in 2009, she wasted no time scheduling me for an ultrasound to see what was going on. Lo and behold, I needed to have another surgery. This time, I had multiple cysts on both sides and a great deal of scar tissue. My doctor looked at me and said, "You know what has to happen, right?" I nodded my head, and not long after, I was back on the operating table. After surgery, my doctor told me that she had to operate on me an hour or so longer than she'd expected because there was so much scar tissue and that I was now in stage four. She informed me that because I was older, the healing process may take longer than it did ten years ago, and she was right! Never did I imagine I would be dealing with physical pain on top of mental and emotional pain.

At this time, I was engaged and getting used to the role of being a stepmom. While I thought dealing with this disease would be a no-brainer, I started to become depressed. I began to think about things that I could care less about before. I began to wonder if I would ever become a mom, if my soon-to-be husband would resent me if I couldn't have children, and so on. I was also going back and forth inside my head whether I even wanted children.

On top of that, issues that I hadn't dealt with in my past started to resurface. Suddenly, I began to miss my deceased dad. I started to resent things that had happened in our relationship. I began to beat myself up because I wasn't where I thought I'd be in my career and life at my age. I was missing some family members that had passed on immensely! Everything started to surface, and I cried about everything. I hated myself and didn't think that I was prepared for marriage like I thought I was in the beginning. I didn't understand what was going on with me mentally and emotionally, so I went to therapy shortly after that. I knew that I was depressed, but I couldn't pinpoint its cause or where these feelings came from.

When I was in therapy, we talked about a number of things, from my family dynamics, to how I was raised, to the things I currently had going on in my life and traumatic experiences from the past. It became evident why all these feelings started coming about. When I was younger, having children was not at the forefront of my mind. I had fun and lived life. Now, I was about to become a wife with a stepson at this time in my life. My emotions were all over the place! I didn't have a great relationship with my father as a child before he passed on. I didn't know if I could have children. I started to feel like less than a woman. Women have a superpower that men do not, and that's the ability to bear children. The words I spoke as a young adult started to haunt me again, "I don't want children." Did I manifest this without realizing it?

My therapist gave me some tips to help me work through all these things I was feeling. I remember she asked me a very, well, what I thought at the time, odd question. She asked me what trauma I had experienced in my life. And for the life of me, I couldn't think of anything. I shared some stories with her about my past, and little did I know, I had experienced trauma in my life more often than I'd thought. Trauma from the abandonment of my father as well as his death. Trauma from my upbringing and past relationships. She made me understand why I am closed off at times and why I feel alone. Everyone around me has children. They may not be married, but they have children, their own little families. It shocked me to realize how jealous I was. I was jealous of my soon-to-be husband having a child and of the relationship they'd formed together. I was jealous of their relationship. It was something I didn't have. I felt like an outsider. I've always felt like an outsider — the friend or cousin with no children. No real family of her own to go home to. The childless auntie. All of a sudden, having my own family and children is what I longed for. It was evident I was dealing with more than I liked to admit.

I had to have serious conversations with my husband to help him understand what I was going through and how I was feeling. We talked about how I felt like an outsider when it came to him and his son. He made sure I felt included more. He came with me to my doctor's appointments to understand my disease better and ask questions.

It hasn't been easy because although we've talked and continue talking to this day about what I am going through, I still have days where I feel down and less than. Be that due to pain or my hormones being out of control and making me emotional. It's still an uphill battle—every single day. I never know if I will wake up in pain or "not in the mood." It's so frustrating, and we are still trying to figure it all out. I know that it affects my husband. He's going through this with me as well as dealing with his own battles. However, he has been my biggest support system.

My stepson helped me heal in ways he will never know. Over this past year, I had the opportunity to be with my stepson for most of his virtual school days. I was working from home, so he and I spent quite some time together. Although I've been in his life since he was nine months old, we never really had the chance to bond one-on-one. We were home all day during this time, so he and I would do his homework and study together, laugh at TikToks, and talk about his favorite games, such as Fortnite and Roblox. I could tell he started to become more comfortable with me by the types of conversations we would have and the kinds of questions he would ask me. Also, the kinds of questions he would ask me. More importantly, was that he was always excited about sharing his good grades or anything dealing with school with me. That's what we bonded over most, his schoolwork. Not until I began to write this chapter did I realize how much he has helped me heal, and I am so thankful. He is smart, athletic, respectful, energetic, and very inquisitive. He was in the top percentile for reading in his class and received nothing less than a satisfactory grade by the end of the virtual school year. I am a very proud stepmama and so thankful that he is in my life! I decided to write him a letter:

Dear Cam,

I don't think I ever told you this, but you have been a major part of me healing the inner "mother" in me. I am so blessed to have been in your life since you were only nine months old. I was there for your first day of school, and I remember when your first tooth fell out. Chipotle is your favorite food, and Fortnite is your favorite game to play. Even though you love your game, you still like to play on the playground and shoot hoops with your dad. Our bond has grown tremendously over this past year. A time when I needed this type of healing the most. You showed me how to be selfless and compassionate. You taught me patience and reminded me how fun it is to be a kid. I am so proud to be a part of your growth, and I thank you for allowing me into your little world. You are funny, witty, smart, respectful, an all-around amazing kid. I pray that our bond grows more and more, and I hope you know I will always have your back, front, left, and right! I don't play about you, kid. I love you much!

Bonus Mom Love:

I DID NOT GIVE YOU THE GIFT OF

LIFE

LIFE GAVE ME THE GIFT OF

YOU.

Your bonus mom,
Ash <3

My mother has also been a big support to me. She has been going through this with me since day one. She's always given me encouraging words, ensuring me that if God wants to bless me with a child, no doctor can tell me no. My mother has been there for me emotionally and physically. By my bedside when I was in the hospital, and my shoulder to lean on when all I wanted to do was cry. Even when she didn't know what to say, she was still there in my corner, ready to support any decision I made. So having her and my husband at this time was so helpful. Having anyone in your corner is always a blessing. Even though they can't change my situation, they made themselves available to me when I couldn't show up for myself.

So, after going to a counselor a few times, I stopped going and started to do my own work. I started meditating, doing shadow work, praying more, and doing daily affirmations. I was in a dark space, and while I understood why, I didn't know how to get myself out of this space. As I stated, my husband and mother were supportive, but they didn't really know what to do either. There was nothing they could do. There was internal work that I needed to do myself to get out of the rut I was in. I knew that I would have to start doing some things differently in order to heal and move on with my life and that happiness is a choice.

At this point, self-help *anything* was my life. I wanted to know how to heal myself if, in the event, I ended up back in this mental headspace. YouTube videos helped me with meditating. I would search for guided meditations on healing and manifesting. I also watched some videos on how to heal yourself. Tips and tricks on how to be happy, etc. This is how I learned about shadow work. I started to listen to self-help books on Kindle and podcasts to see how other women coped when feeling how I felt. I also read and listened to stories from other women who are dealing with endometriosis. I took what resonated with me from all these different resources while praying to God daily to guide me and to put things and people in my path to help me heal, grow, and get to a more positive space in my life.

Sadly, I am still reminded of my disease once every month. And days in between. My doctor and I, to this day, haven't figured out what will work for me to regulate pain. Although I have grown mentally and emotionally, this disease still upsets me. I want to know why. Why me? All because I said at a young age that I don't want children? Who does? This has been the most frustrating thing I've ever had to deal with in my life. Most people don't understand what they can't see, so I don't express it most times if I am in pain. I don't feel like explaining my disease or how I feel, or why I am feeling that way. It truly makes me angry at times to the point of tears. When I think a procedure or medication will work and it doesn't, I get upset all over again. That's when I meditate. So that I can calm myself down, get back to my center and reaffirm to myself that I am not less than. To remind me that my disease does not define me, regardless of how it makes me feel.

Meditating has helped me a lot! I meditate so often now, I've trained my body to stay calm, even in stressful and painful situations. Something I was horrible at before. I used to be an emotional mess. However, meditating allows me to sit still and focus and be thankful that I am still here. It could always be worse. I mainly used mediation guides on YouTube, but I also downloaded an app called *Calm*. This app is for sleep, meditation, and relaxation. *Calm* also offers guided meditations, sleep stories, breathing programs, and relaxing music. This app is great for beginners and truly helps with stress and anxiety.

As previously stated, I also started to do some shadow work. Shadow work is an introspective practice where you work with your inner self, your shadow, so that you may have moments of awakening, which leads to authenticity and emotional freedom. In layman's terms, you take a topic that may be either a trigger or trauma, and you ask yourself about it. Then you elaborate on it and why that situation may still be affecting you today. For example, I asked myself why I don't like change. So, I wrote down what it was about change that I didn't like, what incidents happened in my life that may have caused this feeling, how I feel about change today and how I can handle it better moving forward. This helped me so much. I got many of my topics from YouTube, Pinterest, and Google. When I started, I wasn't even sure what to ask myself. After the first question, though, it opened the door for so many more questions. After about seven questions, I didn't feel the need to continue. When I read over the entries, I realized how so many of my answers sounded immature, but when I thought about it, no matter how immature my answers might have seemed, it's how I felt.

If you are interested in doing your own shadow work, here are some questions you can ask yourself:

1. Think about one time where you felt betrayed. What would you say to the person that broke your trust?
2. How judged do you tend to feel on a daily basis? Explore how much of that perceived judgment is real and how much is imagined.
3. Think of a traumatic experience in your life. How did it change your life? How are you handling this traumatic experience today?

Praying in the shower. That's my thing. I take long showers because I take that time to talk to God. I thank him, tell him what I have going on and what I need help with. I ask for his continued guidance. During this process, I realized just how much God brought me through. At the beginning of this, I was upset with God. I asked him many times why *me* when there are so many other women having children that don't even care for or take care of their children. I thought he abandoned me when I could no longer hear him or even understand what he was doing in my life. I couldn't understand what he was trying to teach me or what I had done so wrong to deserve this.

However, after praying, I realized that He was listening to me and guiding me. I just wasn't tuned in. He had been knocking at my door. I just wasn't answering. I was so wrapped up in the "why" that I never took the time to be still and listen to Him. I didn't just start to meditate and read books on my own. He guided me to these things. I asked God to put the things I needed in my path. To draw me toward these things so much that I know its guidance from Him. During my healing process one day, I heard God say to me, "Bearing children is not your assignment right now; helping others is." While this isn't the answer I was looking for, I found comfort in this answer, oddly enough. Helping people *is* what I love to do! So, if helping people is what my assignment is, that's what I will do.

After some time, I started to feel fine with the thought of possibly not being able to have any children. I wanted to pour more into those that need help, mentally and emotionally. Those that are lost and trying to figure it out, just like I had been doing. So, during the pandemic, I started a YouTube channel in hopes that I could build a community of like-minded people. A virtual community of people that could lean on one another in times of need, give advice, or that could relate to the things I shared. I obtained a Career Coaching Certification, and I will soon complete a Life Coaching Certification. I want to help people heal not just in my community but also anywhere around the world. I started feeling the need to. I didn't know what that looked like for me, and I am still trying to figure it out, so I took to YouTube as my way of starting *somewhere*.

Fast forward to today. How am I feeling? What am I thinking? I am feeling blessed and thankful. Blessed because I am still here. Two surgeries later, I am still here. I realized that even though I didn't have the best relationship with my father, God sent me an amazing husband that loves, protects, and provides. He also gave me a bonus son. Even though I don't have children of my own, I've been in this little boy's life before he even turned one. We've formed our own relationship, and I could not be happier. To see how much he loves and respects me truly warms my heart. I have a plethora of nieces and nephews that I can watch grow. My mother is my best friend. I have a handful of motivational and positive friends and cousins. I have a nice home, a car, a job, and my own little village of support. I am blessed.

When I started to think about the things God did bless me with, I felt ashamed about how I looked at things before. Yes, my health isn't the greatest, but I can still live a life filled with happiness and abundance. Thank God, he didn't take that from me. I started to choose happiness and to start doing things that I love to do. I picked up new hobbies, started doing DIYs around the house, and embraced the new me. I don't ignore the fact that I still carry this disease around, shoot I can't, the pain still reminds me. But I realized having a more positive attitude about it and knowing that every day won't be a great one and that's OK is what's currently getting me through it all. When I have bad days, I let myself have them, but I don't pack up and live there. I get back up because God has an assignment for me. And day by day, week by week, new opportunities keep arising, and I know that it's God's continued guidance and grace, and I am thankful for now being in this place with this new mindset.

Acknowledgements

I would like to thank my other mother, my sister, my mentor, etc. Debbie LeSean for an amazing opportunity! I want to thank you for seeing me and being by my side through some of my darkest times. You came into my life when things weren't going well, and even though you didn't know me well at the time, you still poured into me. You helped me build myself back up. You were a vital piece to my professional growth and now here you are, helping women help other women by telling their stories. You're an amazing person and I am so thankful for you. I am so blessed to have you in my life. Thank you for being you and for doing all that you do. You'll always have a special place in my heart! I love you, Debbie!

Dedication

To my Husband & Mother —

Through the years and all the tears, by my side is where you've always been.

Thank you will never be enough.

I love you!

Reflections

Reflections

III

Rethinking Vulnerability:

RELEASING THE WOUNDS THAT SHAPE YOUR SEXUALITY

Angela Hayes

Angela Hayes is an accomplished public relations leader with extensive expertise in brand development, product lifecycle strategy, nonprofit fundraising, multi-cultural engagement, corporate social responsibility, and cause marketing. She has helped numerous organizations, ranging from grass-root nonprofits to multinational corporations, navigate through major revitalization initiatives by building communications strategies to better position them for growth.

Hayes is a 28-year veteran of the communications and marketing industry. As the senior vice-president of Diversity and Inclusion at Brodeur Partners, she provides strategic oversight of the organization's plans to ensure inclusivity and reach diverse stakeholder groups.

Angela has a whole bunch of kids. She didn't give birth to any of them. They all are her inspiration.

Follow Angela on acollinshayes
 angelacollinshayes ach963

Let's talk about sex and spirituality.

I grew up in a family culture and religious culture that never discussed sex when it comes to women. I come from a long line of ministers and church leaders on both sides of my family. It was fairly common for us to discuss the sexual escapades of the men, including my great-grandfather and father, who were both ministers. These conversations normally took place while talking about an affair. I never recall a conversation that connected the sacredness of sexuality in a meaningful or age-appropriate way. They widely used the moniker "womanizer" to describe the men, which always felt like a way for removing accountability for sexual infidelity. They grew up in a generation where women were shamed and forced into marital relationships for having become pregnant, even when those encounters were not of their choosing — which was the case with my great-grandmother, whose rape at the hands of her employer produced my grandfather.

Despite this, the church has been the pillar of the Black community for generations. Church folks were also averse to discussing sex openly, from my perspective. I remember being taught that sex was a gift from God and that it was nasty and sinful to do it before you got married, but it was fine for married people. Just typing these words overwhelms me with how ridiculous it sounds. Church, in my opinion, should be the place where you can be vulnerable as you learn to integrate sexuality and spirituality. In my case, I was ill-equipped to address sexual issues authentically as I grew into womanhood. As was the case for me, when the wounds that traumatize you as a child are rooted in sex and sexuality, it can take years… almost fifty, as a matter of fact, to peel back the layers of hurt in order to connect with the true divinity of feminine energy that we all carry as women.

Here's my story.

I always thought I would be an actress when I grew up because I found safety in developing and living an alternate identity for as long as I can remember. As an elementary school child, I was fascinated by the story of Sybil: a woman so traumatized by her childhood experiences that she developed sixteen different personalities that required integration. For some reason, I could relate to her.

While I didn't have sixteen different personalities, creating different identities was how I learned to survive as early as age two. My first memory is of being molested as a child. It was during the '70s. My parents took me to a family acquaintance during the day while they worked. This woman was my babysitter for several months before I ended up in the hospital with a traumatic sexual injury.

As I remember my mother telling the story, initially, I loved going to the babysitter's house. I don't remember that part. I do, however, remember in vivid detail how two people, one male, and one female, laid me on a counter and inserted what I believed to be a bear-shaped baby bottle inside my vagina. The man was wearing jeans and a light-colored shirtHisskinwasdark.Ilivedmanyyearsbeingafraidofdark-skinnedmenas a result of this memory. This early childhood trauma would be the beginning of me eating my feelings, protecting myself with layers of excess weight, and developing a mask so that I could fit in while keeping myself and my pain hidden from everyone else.

I was forty-nine before my mother and I ever had an honest conversation about this incident. I remember feeling all the fear and anxiety of that vulnerable two-year-old when I asked my mom, "Why didn't you all ever do anything?" and her response was, "we thought you were OK." I wasn't OK. In my mind, every decision I made in my relationships was grounded in the trauma that I had experienced as a sexually abused toddler.

I was very physically developed as a teenager. By the time I was in sixth grade, I was wearing a DD cup bra. This fact alone made me the target of frequent unwanted attention from older males. Men who my family trusted. Men who were part of the church. Men who should know better than to be making sexual advances towards a fourteen or fifteen-year-old little girl. I did learn some things about sexuality at church: I learned that you weren't supposed to do it until you were married. I learned girls needed to cover their bodies. I learned certain preachers would grab your butt on the sneak tip, so you always had to make sure that an older church lady was around. What I never learned was how to manage everything developing sexually in the context of my spiritual foundation. I recall this creating such conflict within me because I have been aware of my very special connection to God for as far back as I can remember. I often wondered why I was born into this experience without any clear or consistent guidance on how to get through it?

So, in the absence of knowing how to handle sacred sexuality, I started experimenting. In my mind, it didn't really matter — I would never be a virgin because I had been violated at such an early age, so there was nothing for me to "save until marriage." I believe I possessed a toxic mix of low self-esteem and a paternal "hoe" gene that left me with a false impression that the best way for me to be in control of my sexuality was to give it away. Sadly, this approach to my developing sexuality came to a crashing halt one night in the spring of 1996.

I was lying on the couch in my living room, where I had fallen asleep. At around two in the morning, I heard an unexpected knock at the door. It was Jeremy. He was tall, beautifully kissed by the sun, and strong. I had met him at a restaurant near my parents' house a couple of months prior. The chemistry between us was palpable. That was all we had, though. The truth was that I didn't even know his last name. I knew some things about him. I knew he was a Marine. I knew he was from my hometown. But besides that, our interactions were purely physical. Normally, he would call me before coming to my house, so I was surprised to see him that night.

In my disoriented, sleepy haze, I opened the door and let him in. He came in and sat on my couch, and I could smell the alcohol on him.

As I started to wake up a bit more, I got the overwhelming feeling that I might be in trouble. See, Jeremy and I had a very physical relationship. There wasn't anything between us outside of recreational sex. I couldn't have sex with him that night because I had started seeing someone else who I had been with earlier in the day — and that was just out of the question for me. Out of the question.

Jeremy and I sat and had small talk for about fifteen minutes. I asked him what made him stop by at such a late hour. He said that he was in the area at a bachelor party. At that moment, I knew. I knew he was there to have sex with me. I knew I didn't want to. And, I didn't know what to do.

We ran out of small talk. He leaned in to kiss me. I told him I wasn't feeling up to it, and it wasn't a good night. He chuckled, stood up from the couch, and ran upstairs to try to lure me into my bedroom. I got up and walked into my kitchen, feeling panicked and confused, with a million questions running through my head. How could I get him out of my house without making a scene? Why had I opened the door? Where was the telephone if I needed to call someone? What was I going to do? Dear God, what was I going to do? Why didn't I just leave? Yeah, I could do that. I'd just leave.

By the time I had made the decision to leave the house, he was back downstairs, staring me in the face. He pulled me back to the couch and pinned me down. I asked him to stop. He kept telling me to relax.

"Please stop, Jeremy. I really don't want to."

He said something, but I don't remember the words. I just remember that he didn't stop. I couldn't move. I couldn't talk. I couldn't fight. So, I just laid there. Powerless. Crying. The next twenty-four hours set in motion a series of events that were as traumatizing as the incident itself. Police reports. Rape test kit. Having to tell my parents what happened. Telling my parents was hard. Especially my dad.

My personal, early-childhood trauma, coupled with a volatile family life, reinforced some lessons that I would have to unlearn later in life. The first lesson was that you always keep moving forward. Raped as a baby? It's OK. Just keep moving forward. Raped again in your own home? Just keep moving. I learned that I had to find ways to protect myself because despite even the deepest authentic love that a parent could have for a child — as I am certain both my mother and father had for me — there is some shit that no one can protect you from. I learned that while we grow up with certain values and expectations about sexual engagement, things look a little different where the rubber meets the road. I learned that even I struggled to protect myself. So, even as I struggled to protect myself mentally, physically, and emotionally, I became highly skilled at masking the pain that I allowed into my life.

Merging the Sexual and the Spiritual

I lost my power at a very early age through a violent sexual act, so deeply immersing myself in masculine energy was how I learned to reclaim my power. I focused primarily on building my career. I discovered that I was great at shaping public perception and engaging communities. I leaned in on a path in public relations. I had the opportunity to do amazing work and build wonderful programs that were lifesaving. In many ways, my career took off because of an unconscious need to heal the traumatized little girl from my childhood. I started working in HIV prevention and sex education. I would spend years at the local free clinic, walking the streets to teach sex workers how to protect themselves from HIV. I would also work with churches to help local congregations consider sex education as a public health issue, not solely a spiritual one. I built my career on the recognition that there was a point of convergence between sexuality and spirituality. In some ways, even then, I was desperate to remove the mask that kept these two parts of myself falsely separated.

My work was always a safe place for me. If I wanted or needed something in life, I did it myself, with the help of my parents and grandparents. I remember my grandfather telling me, "If a man can't take better care of you than me, then you don't need him." That was a rule I lived by. I never wanted anyone to be close enough to me to really see me, so I would engage in relationships with men that were unavailable. There was also safety in choosing relationships with men who had no desire to have a connection with me. In retrospect, my unconscious preference was for those who were emotionally distant and/or otherwise involved. There was safety in keeping myself masked and not letting anyone get too close to me. In some ways, I think this is what drew me to my husband.

I met my husband when he was a student at VSU, and I was a student at VCU. He was working at a local Mexican restaurant that my girlfriends and I would often go to. What started as a one-night stand evolved into years of an on-and-off relationship until we were finally married. He never wanted to be married, but I insisted on it. We were living together at the time, and I was convinced that his parents would kick me out of the house if anything ever happened to him. In retrospect, this was an irrational fear, considering I owned a home of my own.

Nonetheless, it was a "power" thing for me. They had been very vocal about the fact that they didn't think I was "the right type" to marry their son. And, because I was so deeply rooted in my masculine energy, I was more concerned with proving that I was good enough. So, we got married. This was the foundation of our beginning.

I had been married for two years when my husband was diagnosed with prostate cancer. However, it hadn't been an easy two years together. The mere act of getting married had been full of emotional turmoil and strain. Our relationship changed dramatically after his diagnosis.

For the duration of our time together, our sex life had been a very important part of our relationship. Suddenly our once healthy, curious, experimental sexual relationship was shattered. It was only after beginning the healing process that I could fully understand how much of an impact prostate cancer had on how I saw myself as a woman. And though my rational mind knew that the physical challenges we now faced in our relationship were not necessarily because of anything I had or hadn't done, it felt very personal. Learning to find peace with the rejection and vulnerability I felt following my husband's diagnosis was hard. Prostate cancer also removed the possibility that I could ever give birth to a child.

My vulnerability showed up in my marriage in very negative ways. Mostly as meanness and mistrust. Not the screaming and cussing anger I grew up with, but more of the "I can't look at you without rolling my eyes at you" type of meanness.

Little did I know, I would find my power as I walked through one of the most trauma-filled seasons of my life. In 2017, my brother's children came to live with us, and my mother uprooted her life to move to Virginia to help raise them. In 2018, I launched a new consulting firm after having been laid off. In that same year, my mother was diagnosed with uterine cancer. In 2019, I lost my father, and my mother had a recurrence of cancer. In 2020, I was diagnosed with breast cancer, and in 2021, I lost my mother. In that same year, my baby sister was involved in an incident that almost claimed her life. Add to that the stress of day-to-day life: raising kids, working, trying to have a social life, trying to eat enough fruits, and drink enough water. Life got very overwhelming for me.

I realized in the thick of all that was happening that somewhere along the way, my perception of myself had become filtered through the lens of my accumulated trauma. Even though it looked like I was doing OK on the surface, deep down, I wasn't. I could no longer see myself. My relationship with my husband had drifted to the friendzone. I had no concept of who I was. I could only see what I wasn't. I felt as if I was failing everyone who depended on me — my mother, husband, kids, and clients. The traditional ways of reclaiming my power were no longer viable, so I set forth on a journey to heal my spirit.

There was something very affirming about my breast cancer diagnosis. Having breast cancer was the catalyst that prompted me to take a step back and say, "OK, this is some bullshit. Something has to change." I had just received a "clean" mammogram in December of 2019. By divine guidance, I found the tumor myself while lying in bed one night. It was the start of the COVID-19 pandemic, and I had recently started meditating with Solfeggio energy frequencies as a stress-reduction technique. I rolled over and felt a huge knot. Now, I'm not one to run to the doctor for every little thing, but this one had me concerned. To make it worse, it was the beginning of COVID. I had to go to all my doctor's appointments alone. I couldn't find safety in the church because everything was now online, and people were still trying to figure things out. I still had to care for my kids and my mother. I still had to work to provide for my family. I became acutely aware of all the places in my life where I showed up with a mask on since I hadn't told anyone about what was happening for nearly a month.

Two days after my biopsy, the knot that had felt so huge and pushed me to go to the doctor was gone. From the very beginning of the experience, I felt like God was getting my attention so that S/He and I could start to have a conversation about authentic healing. It wasn't lost on me that the cancer showed up in my left breast, right above my heart. At this time, I began to realize that my sexuality and femininity were so much more than a sexual act. Disease had settled into the feminine part of my body that is designed to protect my heart. I had been heartbroken for some time, and it was as if the cancer was directing me to where I needed to heal. It also wasn't lost on me that I found the cancerous knot in the middle of a pandemic and would need to walk through much of the experience by myself — even the spiritual components.

I did all the conventional things to get myself on the path to healing — I changed my diet and exercise routine, focused more on prayer and meditation, and celebrated the joyful moments that I experienced. For me, the healing that had to take place was so much deeper than the type of spirituality we experience in organized religion. It was as if God was saying to me, "This is between you and me. We are going to use this situation so we can work on our relationship without the filter of outside noise and perceptions." And while I felt myself changing due to some behavior modifications, it didn't fully click until November of 2020.

"I found God in myself, and I loved her fiercely."
~ Ntozake Shange
For Colored Girls Who Have Considered
Suicide / When the Rainbow Is Enuf

The first, and likely most important, step for me to take in order to move beyond the trauma that had shaped my perception of myself was to have the difficult conversations about the things that hurt me. All the work I had been doing to heal started to click one day in November during a conversation with my mother. I was taking her to chemotherapy, and we were having an intense discussion about life. In one of the most vulnerable moments of my life, I found the courage to ask her why she had never pressed charges against the people that had abused me at two. This was hard for me to ask, and I am sure, even harder for her to answer — but she did. She shared with me how things happened from her perspective. She listened as I talked about my memories and how that single event had shaped every relationship I'd been in as an adult. Later that night, as I settled into my reflections, I was able to lay down the mask that I had been parading as masculine energy and just let forty-seven years of pain finally go.

Second, I had to learn to ground myself in gratitude for my wounds to begin to heal. Gratitude, for me, was key to healing. As I began to stop focusing so much energy on my hurt and anger and began to say all the things I was grateful for, my perception began to shift. I could hear the old church mothers singing, "Count your blessings, name them one by one." And trust me, there was power in this for me. I began a practice of taking regular gratitude breaks throughout the day, just to say thank you. During this time, my connection to the Earth also became important to me as a way to ground myself. I would walk in my yard barefoot for long periods. I would integrate amethyst, rose quartz, citrine, and tiger's eye into my prayer and meditation rituals.

Finally, healing began to click for me when I learned to see myself differently. I remember being in a conversation with a dear friend, a person I felt safe being vulnerable with. He wasn't trying to sleep with me. He didn't need me for anything. When we talked, I could just be myself. For many years, he had been a constant and a champion for me. He had the ability to see beyond all my masks, despite how I attempted to hide.

I was telling him about an idea I'd had to do boudoir photos after losing some more weight. He chuckled and asked me why I should wait. I didn't have a good reason. Without missing a beat, he clued into the issue and said, "You don't like to look at yourself. I wish you could see yourself the way that I see you."

I decided to move forward with the boudoir photos. This one act was not only transformative, but it was also the thing that reflected all the work that I had been doing in a way that finally allowed me to see myself. There I was in pictures, looking vulnerable, beautiful, sensual, and sacred. It was what I needed to put to rest and turn the page on the accumulated trauma of nearly fifty years. It would also be the thread that stitched my fragmented pieces back together. For me, there was something profoundly liberating about seeing myself differently. Showing up for myself in this way gave me the strength of heart that I needed to show up as my unmasked self with the people I love.

Photo Credit: Ayasha Sledge of Divine by Design

Acknowledgements

I would like to thank God for choosing me to deliver this message.

I would like Debbie for inviting me to be part of this project.

I would like to thank Freida, Cerdan, Mallory, Cerlisa, Jordan, Nevaeh, Jaron, Tyler, Ellis, Evie and my legion of aunts. I am a better person because of each of you.

I would like to thank my husband, Jeff. We could have never predicted this path, yet here we are. Still showing up everyday.

I would like to thank Sabeen. One of my most vulnerable moments ever was sharing the first draft of this story. Thank you for the care you took in helping this come to life in a cohesive way.

I would like to thank Andy and my entire work family. You have been the light of the sun in the midst of a hurricane.

I would like to thank Nichole M., Nichole H., Jericia, Stacie, Michelle, Angie, Tracy, Shenita, Latara, Renee and Tammy for being in the passenger's seat for this wild ride called life during all different stages of my life. You all are divine feminine energy.

Acknowledgements

I would like to thank Ayasha for seeing something in me that I couldn't see and reflecting it back to me through your camera lens.

I would like to thank my "big brother." You cover me, and I am blessed by it.

And, I would like to thank you. You see straight through me, yet your eyes still speak love to my soul.

Dedication

This chapter is dedicated to my mother. Because of you, I know how to be love. Thank you for giving me the answers, the power, and the courage to be love for myself as well as for my family. I feel you in the breeze. I see you in the trees. I hear the birds chirp, and I know your energy is infinite. I love you, Freida Mae.

Reflections

_____

_____

_____

_____

_____

_____

_____

_____

_____

_____

_____

_____

_____

_____

_____

_____

_____

_____

_____

_____

Reflections

_____

_____

_____

_____

_____

_____

_____

_____

_____

_____

_____

_____

_____

_____

_____

_____

_____

_____

_____

_____

_____

_____

_____

_____

Reflections

CHAPTER

IV

MASKED AT
Birth

Sonya Billings

Sonya Billings was born in the mountains of North Carolina and raised in South Carolina. She currently resides in Virginia. She has a beautiful twenty-four-year-old daughter, whose resilience and beauty has always amazed Sonya. She's currently working toward her Bachelor's degree in Christian Leadership and Management at Regent University. She enjoys living life to the fullest and helping others see their true value. Her goal is to someday open a transition home for battered and abused women and children. In that home, not only will the true love of Jesus be taught but also equipping each woman and child with the tools to see the value of themselves and all it takes to live a free and thriving life in Jesus.

I was conditioned to wear a mask. As far back as I can remember, I was conditioned to hide who I was and all that I was going through. I don't remember a time as a child that I wasn't being told what I should think, how I should act, what should stay hidden, and when I should speak. None of these were my own, but what others gave me. My identity was founded on the instructions of others. The words that stuck out to me the most for years and would make me cringe are: "good girls don't tell," and "good girls don't do this or that." I remember thinking when I was about five, if I'm such a "good girl," then why do I feel this way?

I didn't feel loved or even wanted in the house that was supposed to be home. You see, I was conditioned for abuse and not to see my true worth. The ones who were meant to give me my voice took it away instead and replaced it with a mask. I was sexually abused by one while hated by another. At one point, I had four abusers when I was about five years old. By that time, I felt I was getting what I deserved because I did not know anything else to be the truth in life. I had no idea that I was being conditioned for a life of abuse and just how far it would go. One thing I did recognize is that I was a survivor. No matter what was happening, the will to fight was growing inside of me. However, the will to fight and the ability to fight did not come until many years later. We will get to that later in this chapter.

I learned as I grew up that my mask grew with me. I never seemed to take it off. It was my safe place because, to me, the real me was not worthy of being seen. To the ones on the outside looking in, my mask was beautiful, sweet, perfect if you will, to go with the rest of the masks presented to the public eye. Sundays were especially important as we went to church every time the doors were open. We would put on our Sunday best, and off to church, we went. I found a peace there that I never understood at that time. We sang songs, learned bible verses, and how to obey our parents and the adults in our lives. All the while, I still felt that I couldn't live in truth and honesty because it was forbidden to a certain extent. I was consumed with guilt I didn't quite understand at that time. I was being taught the important lessons in the church: God is love, obey your parents, don't cheat, steal, or lie.

It was a strange form of guilt because it seemed to cause a constant battle within me. I didn't understand why behind closed doors, I was being taught to live life one way and taught in front of others to live another way. I didn't understand, but I also knew I could never ask. Asking questions was seen as being rebellious or disrespectful. I went through life not asking questions for the longest time, which led me to be so naive in so many ways. I did learn that those who were supposed to protect me and teach me the true love of Jesus and who I really was, did the exact opposite. Something I learned along the way, though, was that I should always forgive those who hurt me so easily. For me, that lesson I'd learned so early in church deeply stuck with me. Forgive others so that I could be forgiven. You see, in my mind, I was in such a place of unworthiness that I constantly needed to be forgiven. So, for me, in order to earn God's love, I always had to forgive those who were hurting me.

I went through my childhood, teenage years, and early adult life doing whatever was required to "feel wanted" and be "loved." By this time, I had gotten married and did everything I could to please my husband. I was so young, and to me, it was an escape. I didn't realize at the time that I saw it as an escape. I thought I was in love and knew what that truly meant. We both thought we could take on the world and would be happily together for our entire lives. But I was wrong since we ended up divorcing. This was just another thing, confirming that I was not worthy of being loved. I was conditioned that I needed to sacrifice my thoughts, wants, and body to the point of pain for me to be loved or wanted. If I wasn't in pain, then surely, I wasn't being loved. All the while wearing the mask that made people think I was happy. I was torn and ridden with guilt. I would go to church with my mask on, and yet, sometimes the whole service, I would just weep. I would go to the altar, begging for forgiveness, and get right back up, knowing I wasn't worthy of being forgiven. At least that's what I thought at the time.

I would faithfully go to church, seeking to serve in some way, to earn the love that I was so desperately seeking. Since I was a little girl, singing was my saving grace in a way. As I grew up, I sang in church, in choral, and every chance I got. I didn't understand it until later, but I felt alive when I was singing. I felt truth and honesty were coming from deep within to bring healing to others. My grandfather's favorite song was *Beulah Land*. He would ask me to sing it as a teenager, and he would just cry. It was hard for me because I didn't truly understand at the time why he would ask me to sing it and then cry. I thought I was just hurting him, but in reality, I was bringing thoughts of a place where there is no pain, no hurt, only true healing, and everlasting life. Singing was my escape from who people wanted me to be or how people saw me to who I really was. I started singing in church and seeing God move, not because of me but because of who He was in me. Even then, I still didn't know who I was or who I was supposed to be.

I met my second husband, Simon. He was fifteen years older than me. I was twenty-one at the time, and I was still so very naive. So, when he built me up and told me I was beautiful, I fell for it all. Once I had fallen hard, the tables turned. The verbal abuse and control began. I was back in my uncomfortable comfort zone. To me, I was being loved. My thoughts on how I was to receive love were so messed up. I've learned, many years later, that it came from the conditioning of my life, not something I chose for myself. The verbal abuse turned physical, and for eight and a half years, there were loaded guns to my head, and so many manipulative games played that I just went deeper behind the mask. After all, I was in my second marriage, and surely,

I had to make this one work not to be a failure, yet again. At least, in my mind, I saw it as my failure.

We were blessed with a beautiful daughter, Hannah, about four years into our relationship. By far, this was the greatest gift God has ever given me. The fact that I was married and divorced before getting married again and things were not going well had to be my fault. I never realized I was a victim in the situation. I just believed it was the way my life was supposed to be and what I deserved. In the midst of it all, I continued to go to church, and little by little, God placed people across my path to keep pouring His love into me. I didn't understand, but I felt drawn to Him even more. I wanted to know more. I loved serving and still do. So, I would serve at church as often as possible. I wanted more for my baby girl. I never wanted her to doubt my love for her or to doubt I would be there to protect her no matter what. We all went to church and got involved, but no one knew what was happening behind closed doors.

About eight and a half years passed. By this time in the marriage, I didn't know each morning when I woke up if it would be the day that I would die. We were two weeks into marriage counseling with our pastor. The pastor and his family had left and gone on vacation. I woke up that June morning with a sense of danger in my spirit. I didn't understand it, but I was trusting God to take care of whatever it was. We all got up and headed off to work. Simon was in a strange mood, questioning every word I spoke. It was a long day at work, and I had to come back for a meeting later in the evening. By this time, I kept Hannah as close as possible and kept her in my sight at every possible moment. That sense of danger still lingered so close that I was beginning to get scared. I went to the meeting at work and took Hannah with me.

Before the meeting started, I felt led to call a couple of people from church to get the prayer chain started for our safety and had enough courage to tell them what was happening at home. I was still feeling shame and guilt, so I asked them just to have people pray without telling them why. At that moment, the mask came down just a little. After the call, I put the mask back on and went into the meeting. Team building exercises were the theme. We laughed and worked together, all the while no one knew what was happening in our lives. I had no idea what was about to happen and how everything would change forever.

On our way home that night, I heard a voice just as clear as day saying, "Don't get ready for bed as you normally would. Lock all the doors to the car, except the driver's door, and leave your pocketbook in the car." Now that was a still, small voice, yet strong. I didn't understand, but I knew I had to submit. So, in the house, we went, and I placed the keys right near the door, but kind of out of sight. A few hours later, my baby girl and I cuddled up on the couch and were watching *The Fox and the Hound*. I thought Simon was asleep because as soon as we came home without saying a word, he went to the bedroom. Suddenly, about an hour later, he came storming out of the bedroom and screamed for us to go to the bedroom. Hannah jumped under the covers and hid. Simon went into Hannah's room and destroyed it. Then, he came back and yelled for me. I walked into the living room, and there he was with a knife in his hand. He began to tell me how he had unplugged the phones so that I couldn't call for help. I'd never be able to get away or tell anyone what happened. This went on for about an hour. Needless to say, in my mind, I was thinking, "Lord, you have to get us out of this house. Hannah can't see her momma die by her daddy's hands."

Simon started pacing and swinging the hand with the knife in it back and forth. He had cornered me back into our room. He always made sure I was in a room with no escape when he went into one of his rages. He walked out of the room, and I sat down on the bed. Hannah crawled close to me. I prayed, "Lord, get him into the kitchen, and we can get out." Hannah got into my arms. I prayed, "Lord, get into the kitchen and let me hear the refrigerator door open, and we can get out." Not two minutes later, Simon came into the bedroom and got his glass beside the bed. I knew where he was headed. So, I gathered Hannah as tight in my arms as possible and started easing to the bedroom door open. Then, as soon as the refrigerator began to open, I grabbed the keys while unlocking the door and ran as fast as I could. He came running after us, but I got to the car first, jumped in, and locked the door. Hannah jumped over the seat and started buckling herself in. Simon jumped on the car as I turned it on. I pressed down on the horn, and he jumped off, so the neighbors wouldn't see him, and I took off. By this time, I was crying so hard until Hannah's voice came from the back seat, saying, "Mommy, when are you going to stop crying?"

At that moment, nothing else mattered, other than Hannah knowing everything was going to be OK and that she was safe. The tears stopped, and the mask tightened. We went to my job where I had the key to the door and called the police. That night, with the clothes on our back and no shoes, we stood before a magistrate to get a protective order before going to a safe house. I was so afraid and yet knew God rescued us that night. He had a plan that I could not see. So much changed in some ways that night and, in other ways, got worse. I was filled with a fear that, at times, seemed to leave me frozen. I kept my mask on to protect my daughter, or so I thought. I had to be strong and fearless for her. We stayed in the safe house until I no longer felt the area was safe for us to be. So, I ran to another state, the only place I thought I had to run… to family.

I would love to stop at this point and tell you everything turned around in that moment, and happily ever after came. But, for us, that was not the case. As the years went by, the divorce came, looking over my shoulder became the norm, being in constant protective mode over Hannah became my focus, and the cycle, although it varied, still kept flowing around and around. Those who you would think would be supportive only validated that I got what I deserved and that I was nothing and would never be anything of worth or value.

Oh, but God, He had another plan.

Little by little, I began to dig a little deeper in faith. There was still so much I did not understand. I didn't know you could be conditioned a certain way and no matter how hard you try on your own, the cycle just keeps going. I was learning more about the meaning and depth of God's love, and I could believe anything was possible for everyone else but just not for me. I had the head knowledge but not the heart knowledge. Hannah began counseling, and that was always an option throughout her life. I never wanted my daughter to doubt my love for her and ever to wonder if I would be there to protect her. It was hard to see her hurt throughout the years as her father decided not to be a part of her life. I knew I could never fill that void and that only God could fill that place. There was so much healing and frustration in her life, but that will be her story to tell when the time comes.

The years went on, and in 2010, we moved to Virginia. I was in a relationship I had no business being in because he was not a believer. A month and a half later, I had a car accident that caused seizures, brain, neck, back, and hip injuries. At that point, my life began to change forever. My relationship fell apart. I was out of work, not knowing if I would ever work again.

I shouldn't have been making decisions of any sort. Hannah and I had visited a church shortly before the accident. After the accident, in my mind, if I couldn't serve, I was no longer of any value, and so I stopped going. We ran into the pastor and his wife a few months after the accident at a restaurant. They thought we were just attending somewhere else since we sought a church when we had previously visited. I explained that I had an accident, and I didn't want to be a burden to the church, being so new. They immediately jumped into action, and their daughter-in-law reached out and began to pick us up for church. God started to surround us with very loving people, and I joined a small group, and Hannah joined the youth group.

About six months later, we became homeless, and I was so depressed and filled with anxiety, thinking I deserved this, but not my Hannah. I decided I could lie down and die, or I could fight to survive for Hannah as she was the innocent party the whole time. God opened doors for us, and people stepped up and allowed us to live in their homes throughout the next few years. I was healing in every way physically, mentally, emotionally, and spiritually. Yet, still, I couldn't see my worth. I couldn't look in a mirror and see anything good looking back at me. I still got involved with men who couldn't see my worth. It was uncomfortable, but it was my comfort zone. I kept running back to what I knew. Although I was growing in my faith and would say all the time, "God, I trust you. I know you want the best for Hannah and me," I still wasn't believing it in my heart for myself.

In 2013, I was raped. I went totally numb in the situation. I wasn't physically strong enough to fight back as I was still healing in so many ways. I went into another depression, and my doctor for my brain injury could see I needed more help. I began to see a counselor who helped me understand the brain injury process as well as helping me in all the other areas of my life that needed healing. She no doubt was a gift from God in my life. After about two years, my brain healed to a point, and I had a new ground zero. I could talk clearly, think clearer, make better decisions, finally go back to work, and I began to feel better about life in general. I continued getting involved at church in a great small group as well as a women's group. I was now surrounded by support and people who were pouring the true love of God into my life.

Hannah graduated high school, and I was so proud of her. During her junior and senior years, she began to struggle with panic attacks and severe anxiety and depression. Our relationship had always been open. She was free to discuss anything with me, and it was so important to me for her to know she had a right to her own voice. She saw a doctor and began taking medication to help. That same year, I started having hemiplegic migraines. It appeared to be genetic but was probably caused due to my car accident. No doubt it was yet again another challenge in my faith as I was in so much pain, and it can look like I'm having a stroke when it's a hemiplegic episode. Also, during that time, Hannah began a relationship with a guy from Colorado. He came to visit, and no, this momma did not like him at all because of his self-entitled attitude. But, in 2016, Hannah decided to move to Colorado. I was not happy about it, but I told her I loved her and that, as an adult, she had to make the decision. Now, in that time, I was like, "Lord, you know this guy is not what she needs." I could see in his eyes that he reminded me of the men I had in my own life who were no good. I felt the Lord telling me, "Trust me. Trust what you've taught her about me."

Now, for the first time in twenty years, I was an empty nester. I didn't truly know who I was or what my value was. I still had on the mask, never allowing anyone to see my hurt or pain. I began to pull away from people in many ways and just focus on work all the time. It took me about a year to tell myself that Hannah was not coming back. I started working harder on my relationship with God and healing but still struggled so hard with being valued.

On November 7th, 2017, God placed a friend, a man in my life, who helped me to begin a deep healing process that I had no idea was possible. He treated me with respect and, for the first time, I began to feel loved by a man in a way I had never experienced before. The amazing part is it was through friendship. He had so much wisdom and insights from the experiences that he'd had and was able to pass on so much to me, not just with words but also with action. Although we don't see each other often, the time we share now is always filled with peace, and there is a deep friendship like no other. I began to slowly understand how to remove my mask and become my true, authentic self. There was still so much to learn, but I began leaning more on God while struggling with my sense of self-worth until November 2019.

It was like God leaned in when He placed yet another man in my life to bring a deeper sense of healing. On Christmas Day 2019, my life was profoundly changed. I developed a deeper relationship with Jesus and knew myself more than I ever thought possible. Right from the beginning, we discussed that there would be no games and to be open and honest. This man is a mighty warrior of God and has so much knowledge and wisdom. We knew that we would be in each other's lives for only a season. I learned more about how conditioning impacted every part of my life and who I was. I've been treated with respect, held accountable, and pushed to become who God created me to be. The conversations and lessons have been extremely hard at times. I learned that I had PTSD from the many traumas I have experienced in my life. I also learned that I was in control of myself and the steps to my own healing and self-worth. One of the sayings that he always used was, "You don't know what you don't know until you do know."

Oh, how true that is for me now!

I am now in school to learn about Christian leadership and management. My mask has not only come off but has been crushed into a million pieces. I am now my true authentic self, walking in my truth to be the woman of God He created me to be. I don't look like what I have been through, and now I can help other women see their value and worth as well as to know who they are in Christ. I've always been a fighter for others and have learned to fight harder for myself. My story is now not only being written but also being spoken about. Doors are opening that I never thought would be possible for me. In all honesty, I still struggle, but the struggle has become different. I don't let it consume me, and I quickly remind myself that I am not only a "warrior," but I am also a "queen." No one can take that from me unless I give them the power to take it. I am no longer a victim or just a survivor, but a flower that is blooming to its fullest potential and with a beauty that goes so much further than skin deep.

Acknowledgements

I want to start off thanking Coach Debbie for giving me this opportunity and allowing me to be a part of this project. You have touched my life in ways that will last forever. You are a blessing.

To my daughter, Hannah Faith Billings, you are so fierce and have taught me so much along the way. Thank you for seeing me in the best light even at my worst. I will forever be your number one fan!

To Robert E. Hall @ www.friendsfirst.us, thank you for showing me the gift of "Friends First", a book you wrote and one that still grows me more each time I read it. Your work ethic, your creativity, your love for family and others, and your gifts and talents. You, Sir, are leaving a legacy like no other. You have inspired me to be my authentic self and challenged me to be the best person and friend I can be. I will be forever grateful. You mean more than words can say. A wonderful gift from God. So many heart prints.

To Jerry Russell Jr @ www.iamcognition.com and www.jerryrusselljr.com, for the great headshots and for allowing God to use you in so many ways to teach me so much about myself as well as Him. You have challenged me, pushed me, would not allow me to quit on myself, and saw the gifts and talents within that were just waiting to bloom. You were here but for a season but left a lifetime heart print.

Acknowledgements

To Melodee @ www.joyeofbeauty.com, for doing my makeup for the headshots. You truly gave me the "Queen" experience.

To all my friends and family who have supported me in this life's journey. I will forever be grateful and cherish every moment and memory shared.

Dedication

This book is dedicated to all the girls and women who were never taught how to love and be their authentic self. May you take the chapters in this book to heart and know you are so valuable and worthy of loving yourself so much that you remove the mask and show your true authentic self in your most vulnerable times of pain as well as success and happiness. As an incredibly special friend and author Robert E. Hall told me at the beginning of this writing process, "Write your truth and let your full flower bloom through the process." May you find your path to truth and let your life bloom into the beautiful flower God created you to be. I challenge you to put your truth in writing and write your story and let the healing begin. Take off your mask, there is always another girl, woman watching your life. May you show everyone watching that another "Warrior and Queen, Princess" has taken their rightful place in this world.

Reflections

_____

_____

_____

_____

_____

_____

_____

_____

_____

_____

_____

_____

_____

_____

_____

_____

_____

_____

_____

_____

_____

Reflections

_____
_____
_____
_____
_____
_____
_____
_____
_____
_____
_____
_____
_____
_____
_____
_____
_____
_____
_____
_____
_____
_____
_____

Reflections

V

BREAKING
Generational Curses

Angela Jones

Angela Jones is a native of Richmond, Virginia. She currently resides in N. Chesterfield County, Virginia. She is a wife of a wonderful husband (Weldon), a mother of two beautiful daughters (Akira and Eryn), and a bonus son (Tre).

Angela is a singer and a songwriter of spiritual neo soul music, whose stage name is Ariela Priscilla Baht Israel. Angela has won several awards for her music. In August of 2020, Angela and her husband decided to pursue their dream of entrepreneurship and started First Kings Lawn Care Services LLC. Angela's hope is to one day start an organization to help support Domestic Violence victims.

My name is Angela Jones, and I am a survivor of domestic violence. It took me a long time to come to grips with my personal experience. For many years, I called myself a victim. However, a victim is a person harmed, injured, or killed due to a crime, accident, or other related events. Even though I was harmed physically and emotionally, I fought, and I *survived.*

Growing up, I didn't have a great start in this world. I would see my parents fighting and being young, I didn't know if that was how relationships were supposed to be. My parents would fight, and then, my mother would pack us up and leave. Us consisted of my mom, brother, sister, and I. I was the baby of the family. My sister was ten years older than me, and my brother was eight years older. I remember times when we would go to the house of one of my mother's friends and stay there for a couple of days. However, we would always go back home to my father, and each time, the fights would get worse. It happened so often that when we would leave, I knew that we would go back home after a couple of days. It became a familiar routine.

I recall one incident when my dad and mom were arguing. I remember crying, and my dad picked me up to try to console me. The argument got worse. He then put me down and said he had something for everybody. I remember everyone running. I ran out of the back door and hid on the side of the porch. I peeked around and saw my dad get something out of his car. When he shut the door and started walking towards the front of the house, I started running through the backyard. All I had on was my nightgown. To my surprise, my brother came running and ran right past me. I called his name, but he kept on going. I jumped the gate and was standing in the alley with no shoes on. I looked back and I saw my sister and my mother running through the backyard. I remember my mother yelling, "I'm tired of this!" She began to turn around and go back home. My sister started screaming and crying, begging my mother not to go back. I ran to my neighbor's house across the street and banged on the door. When they answered, I was standing on their porch, crying. As I was trying to explain to my neighbor what was going on, I heard a loud pop. I knew in my heart that was the sound of my daddy's gun. No one was hurt that night. He had only shot the gun in the air to scare my mom. No one knew that it was a warning of what was yet to come.

My childhood changed on August 16, 1984. My mother was finally tired of the fighting and tried to move on with her life. My parents had been separated for about six months. She had found someone who made her happy, and the life she shared with my father was over. My father knew in his heart that she was moving on. He called her and said he wanted to come and get me for the weekend so that he could spend time with his baby girl. She agreed. They made arrangements for my father to come and pick me up.

Later that evening, he came to get me. He didn't have the smile on his face that I was used to seeing; instead, he looked confused and hurt.

My parents went into their bedroom to have a conversation. When he came out, he was upset. He told me to grab my things and, we left. We went to my aunt's house where he was staying. I remember the conversation we had like it was yesterday. My father looked at me and told me that I was the only person in the world that loved him. He said that my mother, brother, and sister no longer loved him. I remember telling him I didn't think that was true. We talked a little more, and then I fell asleep. I woke up a couple of hours later and noticed that he was no longer in bed with me. I went downstairs and noticed the front door was open. I peeked out and saw my father sitting on the porch smoking a cigarette. Unbeknownst to me, that would be the last time that I would ever see him. I got back in bed and went to sleep. Later that night, my sister and brother came home to find my mother and father lying dead in the yard. My father had killed my mom before turning the gun on himself.

My life changed in the blink of an eye. I would never be the same again.

Dealing with the loss of my mother and father as a nine-year-old child left me in a dark place. A place that I don't know if I ever came back from, as I grew into a young woman. I spent my life constantly being reminded that I wasn't anyone's child. Facing things that I should've never faced. I was left vulnerable, even to predators. I remember wishing not to be alive. I would have rather been dead than to feel the pain and anguish that I was feeling every day. I was so angry with my father. I remember feeling as if he didn't even love me enough to stick around. He never considered how detrimental his actions would be for me. However, one thing my mom had taught me was how to pray. That is one of the things that helped me through.

Fast forward to the summer of 1997. I was now living in my childhood house with my brother, sister-in-law, and their son. I was working at a local pharmacy where I could walk to work. One day, I was on my way home from work, and I saw some of my friends. They spotted me and called me over to talk. As we were standing there catching up, a guy that had grown up across the street from me walked over. He instantly started picking on me. He and I had a perpetual hatred for one another. When we were kids, he would throw rocks at me as I played in the backyard. We would argue every time we saw each other. Obviously, this did not change as we became adults. I got mad and walked off and went home.

Later that night, a friend of mine had come over to my house. We were sitting there, bored while figuring out a way to get out of the house. She suggested that I call the guy I couldn't stand from my childhood to come, pick us up and take us to the store. I was like, "Girl, you must be crazy." I didn't want to call him. She then told me that she had done it before, and he always came. So, she called and persuaded me to ask him. When he answered, I asked him to pick us up. To my surprise, he agreed to get us, let us use his car, and pick him up again when we were done. We got dressed, and he was in front of my house within thirty minutes. We got in the car, and he looked at me and said, "Don't have your little boyfriends in my car." We laughed him off and went on about our evening. We rode around, and we had a good time that night. She had to go home, so I dropped her off first and then went back to pick him up.

We began talking and laughed at the fact that we couldn't stand one another, but we secretly liked each other. Later that night, he surprised me with a call. We talked for hours over the phone since we had so much in common. We liked the same music, TV shows, and food. We wanted the same things out of life. It was unreal. We had long conversations every day. He came over and picked me up one night, bringing me to his home, where I met his mom. She smiled as she remembered who I was and gave me a big hug. The next morning, he brought me back home, and we were sneaking in because we didn't want anyone else to know that we were secretly boyfriend and girlfriend. However, that was short-lived as one of our neighborhood friends busted us while walking down the street. We laughed so hard that morning. He was so sweet to me. I thought that I had finally met the man of my dreams. A man that was going to love, protect, and provide for me.

My now ex-husband was such a charmer. Everything that I asked him for, he gave me. We would have a conversation about what we liked, and he would surprise me with them. That was one of the things that I admired about him the most. One day, we were talking about life and everything that we wanted out of it. I wanted to move out of the city into the county. I also wanted to have a black cat with yellow eyes. Sounds crazy, right? The following week, he came over to see me, and he had on a coat. I found it odd that he had on a coat, considering it was still warm outside. I asked him about the outfit, and he smiled, opened the coat, and there was my black cat with yellow eyes. I was so happy! He then handed me a lease for our new apartment out in the county. Soon after, we were in the furniture store picking out new furniture.

We moved in together, and a few months later, he asked me to be his wife. Even though I was happy about everything, doubts were still looming in the back of my mind. I will never forget how I was feeling the day before we were married. I spoke to my aunt, who had raised me, and she instantly knew that I had doubts. I remember what she said before we hung up the phone. She said, "Angie when in doubt, do without." Why did I not listen to her?

A few months later, everything was going fine. We were happy, at least I thought so, anyway. One day, he came home from work with a bit of an attitude and was quiet. We ended up getting into an argument. This wasn't unusual. Couples argue as we had, but this one was different. He grabbed me by my arm and squeezed it so tight that there were bruises on my arm the next day. I went to visit my brother and sister-in-law. She and I were talking, and as I picked something up, she saw the bruises She frowned and asked me what had happened to my arm. I told her the truth, and she looked at me like I was crazy. She then told me not to let that happen again. I didn't think it would happen ever again. I thought maybe he had too much to drink. It wasn't anything out of the ordinary for him to have a few drinks with his friends or after working all day.

Shortly after the incident, we talked about moving to Virginia Beach to get away from our hometown. He had some family that lived there, and they were willing to let us stay until we found our own place. Our lease was up in the county that we lived in, so we moved. The only family I had there was my sister. My sister and I never saw one another because our schedules always conflicted. My ex-husband and I both found jobs shortly after arriving. One Sunday, I was on my way to work, and we got into another argument. This time, he grabbed me again, and I picked up a men's brush with a wood handle and hit him with it a few times. My mindset was like, "Nope, you will not get away with bruising my arm again." Then, I left for work. Still, I kept thinking that this type of behavior was okay.

A month or so later, we moved into our place. Things were fine for a while, but to be honest, it was short-lived. The arguments became more frequent. He was no longer the person that I'd fallen in love with. He had become a different person. He was no longer happy, just distant and angry.

One night, he came home kind of late, after drinking with his brother-in-law and the "garage crew." My brother-in-law and his neighbors would get together on Friday nights to sit in the garage and drink. We got into an argument, but this time he knocked me down on the floor and punched me in the face twice. I got up and went upstairs and cried myself to sleep. I woke up the next morning to go to work. I went into the bathroom and looked in the mirror, and my left eyeball was completely red. The blood vessels in my eye were broken. As I began to walk around, my body felt incredibly sore, so I just laid down in the bed. I thought to myself, "I can't go to work like this." I called in sick that day. However, I had some really good friends who knew my situation, and they called to check that I was doing good.

My ex-husband came home from work and saw my eye. He showed no remorse for his actions. The next day, I went back to work, and my supervisor told me to go home. She begged me to call the police on him. I was in a bad situation and didn't know what to do. I went home and laid on the couch in a state of total depression. My aunt called me, and when I answered the phone, she recognized the sadness in my voice. She asked what was going on, but I denied that anything was wrong. She then said, "Angie, don't let anybody break your spirit. Once that happens, there is no coming back from it." She will never know how those words gave me the strength to get up and fight back.

The next morning, my ex-husband was sitting on the couch watching TV in his boxers. I saw the opportunity to leave. I put on a jogging suit, put all my money in my front pocket, and I ran out of the front door. He couldn't come after me because he didn't have any clothes on. This was all part of my escape plan. As I walked up the street, trying to figure out how to get back to my hometown, Stephanie, a woman I'd met in the neighborhood where my sister-in-law lived, was driving down the street and saw me. How ironic. It was like The Most High had sent an angel to me. She pulled over to say hi and noticed my eye. She asked me what happened, and I told her. I told her that I was trying to get back to my hometown, and she said she would take me. She dropped me off at my in-laws' house, where I assumed I would be safe. However, the words that came out of their mouths proved otherwise. My sister-in-law said that I was painting her brother out to be some kind of monster, and my brother-in-law told me to tell everybody I'd fell. It was the worst. My friend called and said she was ready and took me to my hometown. Not only did she take me, but she also stayed with me for a few days to make sure I was all right. My family members and friends were so mad when they saw my eye. There was no way I could go back, but eventually, I did.

When I initially returned to my hometown, I moved back into my old house with my brother. I transferred to a store that was on the same side of town that I lived on. I was finally getting my life back on track. A few months passed, and one afternoon, I was sleeping in bed after working an overnight shift. To my surprise, I woke up to see my ex-husband standing over me. Barely awake, I asked him, "What are you doing here?" His response was, "I'm here to let you know I love you, and I want you to come back home."

By this point, I was now fully awake. I looked at him like he had three eyes on his face. I stood up and asked him to explain why he thought I'd return with him after what he'd done to me. He apologized and held his arms out for a hug. I hugged him, and I could feel him shaking all over as if he was afraid. I wouldn't be surprised if he were afraid that he would get his butt kicked coming around my family. I got dressed and got in the car with him to go somewhere and talk in private. We ended up at a park not too far from where I lived. He gave me this story about how he wanted his wife back, and he didn't want me to be in my hometown because it was the hood. I told him that I would think about it. I went to visit him a few times in Virginia Beach. It was like we were dating again. Things were going so well that I decided to come back home with him.

Things went well for a few months. Until the arguments started again, it went from small disagreements to intense arguments to physical fights. I began calling in sick from work because my body was so sore, I didn't want to move. I was so afraid to tell my family that I was going through the same things with him all over again. I think that I was more embarrassed than anything else. The only person close to me that knew what I was going through was my best friend, Stephanie. She was with me every step of the way. I would spend time at her house just to get away from him.

One day, our cat got sick and had to be euthanized. He found that to be a good reason for him to drink. I went to Stephanie's house to get away. We were in the kitchen talking when her doorbell rang. It was him at the door. He asked for me, and I went to the door. I stepped outside, and he pushed me as he fussed about me not being at home. So, we got into an intense argument. He picked me up and slammed me in her driveway. Her daughter was twelve years old at the time, and she saw everything. She started crying and calling for her mom. My friend came outside and saw us fighting. She got her baseball bat and got him off of me. She called the police, and he was arrested that night. The police gave me a temporary restraining order. They told me if I wanted it to be more than two days, I could go to the magistrate's office and get an extended one. After two days, I let him come home. Of course, he apologized and blamed his behavior on being drunk. However, nothing really changed after that.

On the night of March 30, 2000, my life would forever change. I woke up to go to work like normal. I had to be there at 11:00 p.m. when I noticed that he hadn't come home yet. I figured he would be there in time for me to go to work, so I waited, but he still wasn't there by the time I had to leave. I called my job and told them that I was running late. I was watching the time, and it was now 11:45 p.m. I started walking to my friend's house to see if she could drive me to work. As I walked, I saw him coming around the corner. I immediately turned around and started walking back. When I got to the house, he was already inside. I ran in, snatched my keys, and left.

I got to the corner, and I said to myself, "I'm tired of dealing with this. This has to end." I turned around and went back. I went inside the house, and I told him I was done. Our argument started, and then the fight soon followed. Somehow, we ended up in the downstairs bathroom. He started choking me over the sink. I reached over and grabbed a razor that I'd used earlier to arch my eyebrows. I closed my eyes, and I started to swing. All I remember next was being on the floor. Not only was I on the floor, but he also had his boot pressing on my chest, holding me down. He was letting the blood that was coming from his hand and wrist drip all over me — in my face, hair, and all over my chest. Even at that moment, I was worried about him being hurt. He finally let me up. The blood was spewing out in streams like in the movies.

I offered to take him to the hospital. We actually got in the car, both of us drenched in blood. Before we could get to the hospital, though, we got into another argument, and he jumped out of the car. I immediately went to my job to let them know I wasn't coming back and to use the phone. I walked in, and my coworker started crying when she saw me. I told her what happened, and I needed to use the phone. I called my brother and told him what happened and that I had to come home. He told me to come on. I drove all the way back to my hometown with half a tank of gas and the clothes on my back.

I got to Richmond, and when my brother opened the door, he looked at me and said, "Is he still alive?" My response was, "I don't know." Later that night, the police knocked on the door, and I was arrested on felonious assault. I was transported back to Virginia Beach the next day. I was told that I had no bond, and in order to receive one, I had to see the judge. The next morning came, and I was called for a visit. There was a lawyer, but hired by whom? My ex-husband. I remember just crying when he told me who'd sent him. It was like I was in The Twilight Zone. I was released a week later on bond, and ultimately my charges were not prosecuted because he did not show up in court.

After the last court date, I remember going to the beach and walking to gather my thoughts. All I could think about was my mother and how I could have easily been her all over again. After returning to my hometown, I went to her grave. I walked up to her headstone, and I said, "Momma, I will not be a victim like you."

Looking back on everything that happened, I see myself for who I really was. When I was with my ex-husband, I was that broken little nine-year-old girl. I was searching for the love that I had missed from my father. So much so that I was willing to put up with being mistreated to get it. I also realized that the world we bring a child into is not the world we know as adults. The world we bring a child into is the world that the parents create for the child. It is very unfortunate that the world that I came into was violent and chaotic, which I considered normal. I put up with a whole lot of things that I shouldn't have because of it.

Deep down inside, I felt as though violence was a way to show someone that you really loved them. Knowing what I know now has given me the opportunity to break that generational curse. I am doing so by bringing my daughters up in a different world. One that shows love and compassion in the right way. Showing them love is so much more than a word that it is an action. Also, that it is normal to have disagreements with your spouse while showing them how to resolve those disagreements. We all have the power to change the future, and I strongly believe that. However, that can only happen if you are transparent, and you take off the mask and expose why we make the decisions that we do. Nothing in life is easy, and no one person is perfect, but you should continue to strive to be the best person you can be.

It ultimately boils down to self-love. You have to love yourself first. You are fearfully and wonderfully made — a child of the living God. You deserve the best. I would like to end this story with one of my favorite Scriptures: "I sought the LORD, and he heard me, and delivered me from all my fears" from Psalm 34:4. I am truly grateful for the strength that God has given me to keep pushing and striving to be a better version of myself. He can, and He will do the same for you.

Here are five survival tips to consider when involved in a domestic violence situation:

1. Pray.
2. Don't keep it to yourself. Tell a trusted friend or family member.
3. Call the police. Never be afraid to contact the authorities.
4. Have a safe word that only you and a trusted family member or friend knows. This will help if you are in imminent danger.
5. Plan ahead. Have somewhere that you can go that is safe for you and your kids, if applicable.

Remember these words from Isaiah 41:10:

"Fear thou not; for I am with thee: be not dismayed; for I am thy God: I will strengthen thee; yea, I will help thee; yea, I will uphold thee with the right hand of my righteousness."

Acknowledgements

First, I would like to thank The Most High God for giving me the strength to endure my trials. Without Him, I am nothing.

Second, I would like to thank my dear friend Stephanie Blount White. You were there for me at the lowest point in my life. If it had not been for your love and compassion, I don't know what I would have done. You were truly sent to me by God. RIP, my dear friend. You are truly missed.

Third, I would like to thank my sister (Kim) and brother (Jake) for their love and support. Kim for being my anchor in a time when I needed strength. Jake for always welcoming me back home with open arms. No matter what and how many times I need to come back.

Lastly, I would like to thank my husband and my kids. To my husband, I thank you for showing me what love and patience are all about. Thank you for supporting me in all of my endeavors and growing with me as I grow. To my children, I thank you for giving me a reason to strive to be a better me for you. I pray that I am the role model that God requires me to be for you.

Dedication

This chapter is dedicated to all of the broken little girls who have grown into broken women. The time is now! You must start to heal. You've been here too long. You are loved, you are beautiful, and you are worth it.

Reflections

_____

_____
_____
_____
_____
_____
_____
_____
_____
_____
_____
_____
_____
_____
_____
_____
_____
_____
_____
_____
_____
_____

Reflections

_____

_____

_____

_____

_____

_____

_____

_____

_____

_____

_____

_____

_____

_____

_____

_____

_____

_____

_____

_____

_____

_____

_____

_____

Reflections

CHAPTER

VI

PRESSING THROUGH

The Pain

Lititca Brown

Baltimore, Maryland native, Lititca is a wife, mother, and grandmother new to the writing scene. She has a Masters degree in Health Care Administration and a Bachelor of Biblical Studies. She loves sharing the word of God with anyone she meets. She has worked in the insurance industry for more than 20 years. She loves to take spontaneous trips and spend time with her family. She owns a small property management company. Her dream is to start an online podcast that will bring families together in prayer. This vision started to flourish in June, 2019 when she started a family prayer line with her family. They are going on 3 years strong! Her go-to scripture is Proverbs 3:5-6 (NIV):

"Trust in the Lord with all your heart
and lean not on your own understanding;
in all your ways submit to him,
and he will make your paths straight."

Life, Love, and Happiness

I was coming out of one of the most painful experiences in my life. Before getting married, my husband was hit with a tragic situation that cost him everything he worked so hard to obtain. It was devastating seeing him suffer while I could not help him. He was strong, he held on, and God saw him through all the pain and suffering. By the grace of God, he recovered everything. My mom passed during this time, and coping with her no longer being with us took a while to heal. I needed time to heal. I can still remember that day like yesterday, but no longer seeing her suffer was priceless. She was a gem, a fighter, the mother of twelve beautiful children. And, most of all, she was our strength. She taught me how to be strong and fight despite what I was going through in life. She was my backbone. When faced with obstacles, she told me to keep praying, and it would all work out in the end.

A few years later, I married the love of my life, my soulmate, and, together, we have a beautiful daughter who is my heartbeat, my reason for never giving up in life. We were finally a family, and all our troubles were behind us. We loved traveling, taking spontaneous trips to New York, D.C., and our favorite place, Cowtown. My daughter was in her sophomore year of high school, and she was on the volleyball team. My husband and I were actively involved at her school. I was vice president of the Parent Teacher Organization (PTO), and my husband ran the concession stand. The kids loved his hotdogs and hamburgers. Life was just starting to move in the right direction, and I was happy.

The Diagnosis

Things seemed to be on track, so I thought. Then came the dreaded day when I found myself in so much pain that I ended up at Patient First. It was April 2015, one of the most devastating days of my life. I thought it was a urinary tract infection because the pain was familiar to what I experienced in the past. I called my husband and told him I was on my way to Patient First, and he asked if I was OK and if I needed him to meet me there. I said no, and asked him to go home to make sure that my brother, who'd come to live with us after my mom's passing, was fine. He was in an adult day care program and needed assistance getting on and off the bus.

I signed in and waited for my name to be called. They called my name about thirty minutes later, took my temperature, weight, and height. The nurse asked where I was hurting. I pointed to the section of my body where I was experiencing the pain, and she asked for a urine sample. This was nothing unusual. I have been here before, so I thought. I provided the sample and then proceeded to my assigned room.

It took a long time to receive an update, but I didn't think anything about it. She came back about forty-five minutes later, saying they needed to take some blood. That's when I got a little worried and wondered, "Lord, did I wait too long? Did I allow this minor situation to get worse?" They never took blood before for a urinary infection. Whatever they saw could not be good. Why did they need blood? My mind was running all over the place, thinking the worse. The nurse came back about forty-five minutes after taking the blood and asked if anyone was with me. I replied, "No, what's wrong?" I started thinking of every possible illness: cancer, a deadly disease, anything except a UTI. Yes, I was in pain, but it wasn't hurting that bad. I started downplaying my pain, thinking if there's no pain, then there's no issue.

The doctor came into my room, asking who they could call to be with me. They would call the ambulance so I could go to the emergency room right away. I said, "Hold up, wait a minute. What do you mean, call the ambulance?" I was thinking, am I dying? Now things really got real. What was going on? The doctor informed me that I was losing a very high protein level, and my creatinine levels were extremely high. "We need you to go to the emergency room ASAP." What? What is creatinine?! What do you mean my levels are too high? At this point, I was looking for an answer, and I swear I forgot all about the pain.

I requested to call my husband. I refused to go anywhere in an ambulance. I told the doctor my husband would come and take me. They agreed but pressed upon me to go that night. I called my husband, he picked me up, and we headed straight to the ER. When I got in the car, I started telling him about my issues, and he got this look on his face. He did not say anything, but I knew he recognized the terms because he'd worked as a firefighter and an EMT operator for years. I wanted him to tell me it would be OK, but all he said was, "Let's wait and see what's going on when we get to the ER." Now, that was not what I wanted to hear, as you can imagine at this point. I wanted him to tell me that I was fine.

When we arrived at Mercy Hospital, I gave them my name. They immediately took me to a room and started taking my vitals, and gave me IV fluids. By this time, I was in a panic mode, not knowing anything about creatinine.

This would be the beginning of my journey, my battle for life, love, and happiness.

Never in a million years would I have thought this would be a road I would travel. Even though my husband was there, I felt completely alone! Yes, I felt alone. I knew something was wrong, and all I could think about was my baby, who was away at college by this time. How could I tell her that I was sick? Who would be there for her? Would I miss her life, her getting married, having children, and buying a home? How could this be happening to me?

So many things were running through my mind, I forgot who I was, and my foundation laid by my mother: I forgot to pray. I lost focus and had more questions than answers. The doctor came in later and began to tell me what was happening. He stated that the high level of creatinine was impacting my kidney function, and I would need to see a urologist. It looked like I had a small blockage, which was causing most of the pain. They also gave me fluids because I was dehydrated, but I could go home. As the doctor was speaking, my husband asked what the levels were and if the fluids would help. Again, I could see that look in his eyes. I knew that he understood what was going on but wanted to be optimistic.

I could not understand how he could be so calm at a time like this, so I tried to be calm since I did not want to let him see me break down. I was a nervous and emotional wreck on the inside, but I was trying to look strong on the outside. Honestly, I was beyond upset, angry, and ticked off; you name it, I was feeling it at that time. The ER physician set me up with an appointment to see a urologist. As we drove home, my husband tried reassuring me, saying, "Don't worry, baby. It's going to be OK."

Emotionally, at this point, I wanted to be left alone. I knew the kidney was a vital organ in my body. Someone telling me that it's going to be OK felt like throwing salt onto the wound. I know he was trying to help, but it was not what I wanted to hear. If someone had told me that I would be confronted with a life-changing situation that I could do nothing about, I would have called them a liar! Over the next few days, I would wait for the appointment with the urologist. Would this be an answer to my pain?

The Search for Treatment

The day of my appointment arrived, and I wished I had someone with me. But I was trying to handle it all, telling myself I got this, and I was all alone. The doctor called me back and began asking me all sorts of questions. Have you ever been diagnosed with lupus, high blood pressure, or diabetes? I was like, "Come on!" I just wanted the doctor to get to the point already. Who wants to hear about his research that diabetes, high blood pressure, and lupus are leading causes of kidney failure in the African American population? None of this applied to me. I was feeling insulted and pissed off. A million things were running through my head, and a history lesson was not what I wanted to hear.

He ordered an ultrasound, and the results indicated that there was a blockage. I had a moment of happiness, thinking that a blockage could not be that bad. The doctor said that placing a stent may help decrease the creatinine levels and some of the pain. Hearing that news allowed me to breathe again. I thought I was out of harm's way. I got an appointment two weeks later to place a stent in my bladder. I had to press my way through the pain over the next two weeks, but this was a different kind of pain.

Nevertheless, I dealt with it by working and going to church as if nothing was wrong. Lord knows I was in so much pain. Two weeks went by, and, to my surprise, the creatinine levels did not change. I was referred to a nephrologist who wanted to start dialysis three days a week immediately. My husband said we needed a second opinion.

I began to worry about my job, finances, and if my family could make it. We were a two-income household, and our daughter was in college, so money was tight. How could I do three days of treatment and work at the same time? So much was going on, and I had not even told my daughter. I was still caring for my brother, trying to make sure that he was fine while taking care of myself. It was difficult with his dementia progressing. He was becoming confrontational, didn't want to listen or even bathe himself.

My patience was wearing thin as I was dealing with my situation, and I was beginning to feel like I was letting my husband and daughter down. I continued to search for answers and look for help. I was referred to a doctor in Columbia who was supposed to be really good. I will never forget this lady's face. The questions she asked me were offensive right from the start. "Why are you here? I see you are in stage three kidney failure. You know it's irreversible at this point; there is nothing we can do unless you lose weight."

I got the feeling that she would not be of any help to me. She went on to say that she was not sure what else I wanted her to do except start dialysis, live my best life, and enjoy my family since getting a transplant was not an option because I was overweight. What the hell! By this time, I was almost in tears and could not wait to get out of her office. I called my husband, crying and upset because this lady was saying to start dialysis as there was no other choice or treatment for me. She made me feel like I was wasting her time. Can you imagine being told there is no hope for your situation? Just thinking back to that day brings tears to my eyes!

My husband said, "No, we won't accept this diagnosis. Don't listen to her, and we'll get another opinion." I called my primary care doctor, asking for a referral to see another nephrologist. She gave me a list of doctors. I came home and researched each of them. I began to pray and ask God to give me someone who could help me. I started falling into a depressed state. Yes, me, the strong one in the family, the believer of Christ. I was losing all hope. I tried to hold my head up with a smile, reminding myself that I got this, but I was in pain deep down inside, and I was angry. I was asking God, why are you allowing this to happen to me? I tried to do right by people, and I know I am not perfect, but Lord, I don't deserve this. Funny how we tell the Lord what we don't deserve!

So, now Lord, what do I do? How do I take care of my family and brother when I can't even take care of myself? I found myself praying and asking for a doctor who would give me answers. After looking up several doctors, I found Dr. C. I called the office and scheduled an appointment. He did his assessment and said, "You are pretty healthy.

I do not see any trend in your creatinine levels from the past few years. I am not sure why your kidney is failing. Let's get a biopsy and start you on medication to see if we can stop the increase in the levels."

He started me on prednisone. If you don't know this medication, it's horrible because your body just blows up. We started this treatment, and I started gaining a lot of weight, which became depressing. I went from a size eighteen to twenty-four within months. We tried multiple medications. Whatever he suggested, I tried.

The biopsy results came back, and there was damage to the kidney. I was diagnosed with focal segmental glomerulosclerosis (FSGS). Dr. C told me that there was not a lot of information on FSGS or how it starts. He pointed out in my case that it may be genetic. Both of my parents were deceased, so I had no one to ask. No one in my family was ever on dialysis as far as I knew.

This result worried me on a different level since I immediately wondered if my daughter would someday experience the same fate. At this point, the drugs were not working. I had to find the strength to tell my daughter because I wanted her to be aware of the signs. If there was early detection regarding this disease, I wanted her to know about it. Telling her became crucial.

After telling her, she wanted to come home, and I denied her request. I needed her to finish school first. We were now nearing March 2016.

A year had passed, and we had tried everything. Dr. C was increasing the prednisone, and I was getting bigger and weaker. I was still trying to fight through the changes. I was praying for a breakthrough, but nothing was happening.

There were issues with my husband since I was feeling unattractive, and intimacy was off the table. I began to wonder if he even loved me anymore. He never said anything or complained, but I was feeling different. I wanted him to hold me, but I didn't want him to touch me. I knew it was me. I was in a lonely space, and no one understood my pain. Not even the love of my life. I was hit with the final truth that all options were exhausted. My doctor said I had no other choice but to start dialysis. I was upset, depressed and knew my life would never be the same again.

Research and Treatment

By September 2016, I was referred by Dr. C to a treatment center called Fresenius. He sat me down and told me that dialysis was not the end of the world, it's a start to feeling better, and I could be taken off some of the medications. He told me there was another option if I started dialysis and did well. I found out that by starting this treatment, I would be eligible for a kidney transplant. He said that I was a good candidate because I was pretty healthy without any underlying conditions. Yeah, right. Healthy! If one more person told me that I was healthy, I would scream. If I was so healthy, then why in the world was I here?

I was getting acquainted with dialysis and knew nothing about transplants. I first needed to learn as much as I could about dialysis. What was the process? What would I need to do? And how often would I need to do it? The doctor recommended two options; both had pros and cons. Hemodialysis was administered three days a week, and peritoneal was daily. How do you select the right treatment for yourself?

The Emotional Roller-Coaster

This was becoming an emotional roller-coaster, trying to make the best choice of treatment. I scheduled an appointment to review the films provided by the clinic to help make my decision. After watching the films and seeing what happens during the treatment, I became an emotional wreck. I was crying the entire time I was alone, scared, and confused. All I saw was a machine with multiple cords. How could this be my only means of survival? I thought life as I once knew it was over. No more spontaneous trips in my future. All I saw was a lifetime of unhappiness.

I would have permanent scars either way, and life would never be the same. I no longer felt beautiful. Would I ever want to be touched and caressed again? Would I enjoy making love as I once did, or would my current situation always be in front of me and overshadow the things I once loved to do? Would my husband remain faithful through this process? Tears rolled down my cheeks in fear of the unknown.

My baby girl was now a junior in college. She called to check on me every day. I was so down some days, but that phone call was my ray of sunshine, my joy in the middle of this storm. For a while, her calls made me smile as I would listen to all her new adventures in school. She was having the time of her life, which gave me joy. She was my motivation to push through my pain. I wanted to see her graduate, get married, and have children. The thought of not being there for those milestones in her life was devastating. So, I had to press through my pain if I wanted to enjoy those moments with her.

My husband took me to my first appointment at the treatment center. I saw how his heart was broken when he watched all that I was going through. He looked as if he wanted to break down, but he would never let me see him broken. They mentioned to him how the treatments could be done at home. I said no, I did not think that was a good idea, and he said he would do whatever I wanted to do.

I was later injured during a treatment session, which made my arm swell badly due to an infiltration of the vein. My husband was distraught, and this caused a major setback. My husband asked me to reconsider treatment at home. I agreed, but with much reservation. He took one of the rooms in our home and turned it into a treatment room. I came home from my treatment one day, and he surprised me with everything I needed to administer those treatments at home. It was at that moment that I knew this man loved me beyond life. He wanted me to be home; he wanted me to be comfortable and would do anything to make that happen.

Because of this act of love, I knew I would have the support I needed. I asked nurse S. to help train me, so I knew what to do. She was the best nurse at the facility. There was still a question about being listed for a transplant. Nurse S. asked me to please get on the list as I would never know what God had in store for me until I did it. I told her that it hurts my heart to know that someone else has to die in order for me to live. She reminded me that I was worth it and I had a lot to live for. Plus, those on the donor list do it for that reason, to save someone else. She said if I never took the steps, I would never know what God will do. She urged me to go through the process, and if I got a call for a kidney and didn't want it, I could always say no.

I prayed about it, discussed it with my husband and daughter, and they both agreed that I should get on the transplant list. I completed the process and was placed on it right away. They both wanted to get tested to see if they were a match, but I had reservations about my daughter giving me a kidney as she had no children at the time, and I did not want to rob her of that chance. I did not know if this disease was genetic, and that was not a risk I was willing to take with her life. My husband got tested and was a match, but my fear of the disease being genetic led me to tell him no! What if our baby needed a kidney in the future? The fear of the unknown and not understanding my options was the worst feeling in the world. I learned that you have to do your own research by searching the Web and learning whatever you can when faced with a life-changing situation.

My husband and I were both trained, and my home treatment began. At first, it was a rocky road between making the solution every other day and the pain of sticking myself with those huge needles was more than I could bear. But I had to do it to survive. Despite injuries, blood clots, and reconstructive surgery, I was able to give myself the treatment.

My baby graduated from college, and this was a happy time for my family. I had tears of joy that day. Seeing her walk across the stage was priceless. My treatments were going well, but I still felt like I was a burden to my family. My husband or daughter had to rush home from work to help me with treatments. I felt like their lives were put on hold because of me. This was all becoming a strain, and I refused to ask for help or tell them when I felt terrible. I knew this frustrated them because they knew I needed help. After voicing their frustration, I realized they loved me and would do anything for me, but I had to get out of my own way. It was a process!

Remember my brother who was living with me? His health was fading. I found out he had terminal cancer, and this was a blow to my family. My mood swings were getting worse. Some days I was happy, some days I was sad, and some days I was angry. I was praying and going to church, looking for answers. Any answer would do, but I was not receiving anything.

It Is Well

One Sunday morning, it all changed. It was during morning worship when the song It is Well was sung. It was at this point that I totally surrendered my soul to God. I told him to take away all my hurt and pain. I made up my mind that day that there was not a single thing I could do about my situation except to pray. My prayer began to change as I started praying and confessing to the Lord that whatever Your will is for me, I will be satisfied. At this moment, I realized things in life would happen that I would have no control over. As a believer, I had to shift my thinking process. I had to trust God in my process. I had to press through the pain and dig deep down inside to find that mustard seed of faith to keep pushing on. I had to believe in the verse in Hebrew 11:1: *"Now faith is the substance of things hoped for, the evidence of things not seen."* I learned it was OK to cry, OK to say I was hurting, depressed, and needed help. Through mental, physical, and spiritual pain and suffering, I discovered it was OK not to be OK. I was learning to press through my brokenness despite my situation. I was a child of the King. I was wonderfully made, and I was going to fight for my life.

I knew that if God chose to heal me at this point in my journey, it would be well, and if he did not choose to heal me, it would still be well. Either way, I was going to give him thanks. In 1 Thessalonians 5:18, it says: *"In every thing give thanks: for this is the will of God in Christ Jesus concerning you."* It was then that God began to move on my behalf, and I started to live again. My life of prayer changed, and so did my relationship with God. I was developing a closer connection with God. Instead of asking God, "Why is this happening to me?" I began to hear him say, "Why not you?"

God reminded me even though I may be down; I am not counted out. I still have much to give. In turn, I began to pray for others. I understood better the story written about the woman with the blood issue. She spent all the money she had looking for a cure! It was not until she put her faith into action and reached out to touch the hem of his garment that she was healed. As stated in James 2:17: *"Even so faith, if it hath no works, is dead, being alone."* I had to do my part and push through my situation, even if it meant sticking myself with a needle and being on a machine four days a week. I would do it for my family. I began to trust God fully, and my faith was restored. It was well with my soul! I began to lean not on my own understanding but in all my ways acknowledged who God is and trust in his word as mentioned in Proverbs 3:5-6. I went back to doing things I loved in the church and life. Things were a little different, but I tried to make the best of it.

Dealing with my brother's diagnosis was painful, and I did not want him to suffer. I asked God to give him peace and not to let him suffer. I took the focus off myself and began to focus on what I could do for him instead. In September 2018, there was nothing else I could do but make him comfortable. I was able to set him up in a hospice. They came in and played music for him, prayed with him, and for a moment, knowing that he was a little comfortable was a relief.

I found out during all of this that my daughter was going to have a baby. I was so happy for her. What I had once feared was no longer in front of me, and I would be here to witness the gift of life. Words can't explain how overjoyed this made me. Even though I was getting weaker and tired, I was overwhelmed with joy knowing I would see her finish college, have a child, and be employed at a good facility. She was dating a wonderful young man who later became her husband. This was a good moment in my life despite what I was going through. I had a glimpse of happiness once again.

In October 2018, I received the long-awaited phone call that a kidney was available. To my surprise, it was from a living donor. Can you imagine how ecstatic I was? No one had to die! Hallelujah! Hallelujah Amen! I started to cry because I knew that in my heart, God had heard my prayers. I would go through a series of tests before the transplant would take place. One test came back positive, however, which delayed the process. The delay was like receiving a bad diagnosis all over again. Just for a moment, the enemy tried to get me to doubt my blessing, but I started to pray. I called on the prayer warriors to help intercede on my behalf.

During this time, my brother's condition got worse, and he was heavily on my mind. I called the nursing home to check on him to see how he was doing. I could not visit him due to the risk of getting exposed to infections, which was difficult for me. I had to rely on my family to relay information regarding his condition. On October 30, the same day I received the all clear to move forward with the transplant, I received the call that my brother passed away. I remember crying. On the one hand, I had received wonderful news that I was approved for a transplant, but on the other hand, devastating news that my brother was now gone.

My transplant was scheduled one week after my brother's death. I believe God allowed the false diagnosis of a potential nodule on my thyroid to delay the transplant so that I could bury my brother. God knew if my brother had passed after my transplant surgery and I could not properly bury him, I would have been crushed. God knows our hearts and, he hears our prayers.

Going through this process has allowed me to realize several things. I realized I am not a superwoman; I am vulnerable to life's changes. When we are emotionally, physically, and spiritually broken, we lose our way. We become entangled in our own needs, which hurt others, and we do not even realize it. We fail to see the beauty that life has to offer. I am blessed with a wonderful husband, daughter, and family. I saw my husband pray a little differently, love differently, and he never judged me despite all the changes I went through and still must go through. I know now, without a doubt, this man would do anything for me. Our relationship grew, and we became closer and found a new love for each other. God allowed me to see a new life in the birth of not one but two beautiful grandsons, and I am so grateful!

My Takeaways

Through all the pain and suffering that I have experienced, I now know it is OK to ask for help, which does not mean you are weak. I learned how to pray on a different level. I pray, expecting and looking for an answer. The answer may be a no, but sometimes it's a yes! I received that yes on November 8th, 2018, when I was given a second chance at life. When going through difficult times, never accept what anyone else tells you, do your research and trust God in the process. God is listening, and he hears our prayers. My life of prayer with my family changed. I learned there is power in prayer, *but even more power in family prayer*! Look for more to come, how to bring your family together in prayer, and watch God work for you!t

Acknowledgements

I am forever grateful To God for giving me a second chance at life.

I would like to acknowledge my donor who unselfishly gave me this gift.

To my family, friends and church family; you were my village in the time of a storm. You carried me in prayer throughout my process and still today. I am forever grateful for your love and support!

To Lady Bragg & Michele Defoe thank you for the late nights just to make sure I had my thoughts right.

To Sean and Tamekia, "team duo," for the photographs & make up.

To Bishop & Lady Pender thank you for lifting me up in pray during my darkest hour. Your phone calls and words of encouragement will never be forgotten.

To my son in-law Q who jumped right in to help thank you for your support

Dedication

I want to dedicate this chapter to the love of my life, my husband Eric, and my heart beat, my beautiful daughter Jada. I would not have made it without the both of you. Thank you for loving me and never giving up on me even when I wanted to throw in the towel. Thank you for being there every step of the way. You never missed a beat! I love you with all of my heart and words will never be able to express the love I have for the both of you. To my grandbabies who bring joy and happiness to my heart GG loves you.

Reflections

_____

_____

_____

_____

_____

_____

_____

_____

_____

_____

_____

_____

_____

_____

_____

_____

_____

_____

_____

_____

_____

Reflections

Reflections

_____

_____

_____

_____

_____

_____

_____

_____

_____

_____

_____

_____

_____

_____

_____

_____

_____

_____

_____

_____

_____

_____

VII

THE
Four Walls of
Wonder Woman:

PROTECTION, SECRECY, DEFIANCE, AND POWER

Shana Williams

Shana Monique Williams is a Charleston South Carolina native. Dr. Williams loves being a nurse and doctoral prepared Psychiatric Nurse Practitioner. She is passionate about care and engagement of those experiencing behavioral health illnesses and a part of a collaborative team who impacts the future of the nursing profession." Shana currently lives in Durham, North Carolina with her two sons Christopher John and Shane. She enjoys spending time with the love of her life, her family, fellowshipping with friends, reading, watching movies and walks in the park. She is kind of a fun nerd!!!

Her philosophy is: I love people and making sure that everyone I come in contact with has the best life.

Rape, pregnancy, and loss of self all before the age of nineteen years old. Great parents, great sister, great cousins, and great friends. However, I felt like I did not feel protected. Not because my parents did not try, but someone I trusted deeply abused my trust with one forceful penetration. My safety was violated with the biting of my breast. The construction of my first wall, called "protection," was complete when he, "the evil villain," decided to explore my rectum until I no longer felt like our friendship was genuine or loyal. How did a friendship I once cherished change in one day? He used to make me feel safe, and he invaded my camp…

I felt unsafe, and seeing him at school made everything about my senior year worse. Each day, he talked to me, reminding me of the horrible moment when he took my voice, my identity. Not even one month later, I figured out I was pregnant, and the construction of my second protective wall began. I needed to protect "us" from him and his evil ways. I had almost two walls in place. That should be enough, right?

"If I move in silence, no one will notice." Every month, I looked for ways to keep my secret and build my wall. I made it to graduation and left for a summer program at college. No matter how many bricks I put in place, however, my secret was getting harder to hide as there was this small human that I love deeply growing and thriving despite the way he was created. I had to tell someone I trusted, but how could I? I had to tell someone, but I was so afraid of their judgment. What if someone told him? Our tribe was tight, and certain things were not tolerated. So, let the next chapter of life begin.

Summer school consisted of nosy girls who wondered why I wore such big clothes. Guys were not appealing to me as I did not trust anyone. I was angry, sad, disappointed, and just empty. Yet, a small human continued to grow and thrive to the point where I broke down one day and told my mom of the day the first wall was constructed. We then, as we always do, sat down as a "fantastic four" to talk about what I needed from my family. They were willing to keep my secret at any cost, and I had their full support to walk through this journey. Many questions were asked: Did I want to keep the small human? Did I want to return home? How did I feel about remaining on the college campus? Luckily for me, no one ever asked who it was…

The doctor appointments started, and off to therapy, I went. Yet, I excelled in summer school while hiding from my roommate and the other girls in the dorm. I was proud I made it through summer school with my secret and the small human safe. Yet, I faced another challenge. I was going back to the one place I dreaded, which I used to call home. How would I adjust in the place that was now such a bad memory, symbolizing a lost friendship and the loss of myself? He also figured out I was home and inquired about what was going on with my stomach. The construction for my second wall became complete when I was no longer allowed outside of the house due to questions from the church, family, and friends around town who wanted answers. As a family, we made an agreement, and I knew what I had to do. The construction of my second wall, called "secrecy," was complete, and seclusion began until my life and first of two heartbeats decided to make his appearance.

The month of October 1998 was when my life changed forever. On October 3rd, the pain flooded my body as the small human was preparing to see the world. So many emotions were flooding through my body with each contraction until my first heartbeat was born on October 4th, 1998. I felt so much love and peace, but at first, I did not want to see him. Yet, the nurse came in with pictures, and the second wall began to crack until I was filled with love and peace. After many hours, I asked the nurse to see him, yet I was so wrecked from thoughts about how he looked, and what if I could not keep my end of the family agreement?

He was so beautiful and looked nothing like "the evil villain." He was so soft, and he knew me immediately. I stayed up all night and talked to him as we had to share so much for me to keep the agreement made with the "fantastic four." The next morning came, and it was time for me to leave, and the agreement of giving him up for adoption had to be kept. The love I had for him turned into hurt, and the peace I had turned into anger. I began to construct and complete my third wall, called "defiance," as I walked out of the hospital without my first heartbeat with the plan to "continue my life plan my way." Oh, but I was so broken and angry... It would be that way for a long time until I was ready. The wall needed to be up since no one could enter my camp and take away anything else from me.

In January 1999, I decided not to go back to the college I once thought was my foundation because I was broken and being a defiant "grown-up." At a new college, I was determined not to let anyone in or infiltrate "my wonder camp." The goal was the following: look unattractive by wearing the biggest clothes and cap I could find, go to class, not talk to anyone, and not date anyone. I also figured I would need more armor to be prepared for this stage because I had to be ready for anything that came at me, including a charming man! I knew he would be tall, and I would not see him coming. I also had to be cautious as I was broken, mean, and just not enjoying life now.

But my kid was gone. I had no idea where he was, and as I was taught, you only have one life to live. I had a goal of becoming a doctor and impacting lives. Being at this college was a good start. It was supposed to be a new start, like a reset to where I would have been if I did not sit out the semester to have a baby that no one else but five people knew about. I could not even bring myself to leave my emotional camp, and I now picked up my crown, bracelets, and swords to maintain my safety and continue constructing my "defiance" wall. I did not want to be angry forever. When I stepped on campus, I was approached by many, but I had no one to keep me safe and who knew about how protective I was over "my wonder camp," so I decided not to stay on campus but at home where it would be easy to meet my goals.

For months, I went to class, sat in the library in between, did not interact with anyone, and took my butt home when class was done for the day. I only hung out with the "one that kept me safe and protected." Until one day, someone asked me a question about my big clothes and cap. The wall of "defiance" was almost complete, and he would not get that answer. I told him, "Leave it alone," and walked away. Yet, when I noticed him again, he was in my maths class, he started coming to the library and, before I knew it, he asked for something simple... Help. Who was "the one who pulled himself up by his bootstraps, also known as Mr. Bootstraps?"

I have a heart, a tremendous, big, did I say, huge heart. He needed help with the class, and I understood everything, so why not? I broke my first goal of not talking to anyone then. I began to help him with maths, knowing that he was brilliant and knowledgeable. I was not going to break any other goals as he was not what I needed right now. The more I got to know him, I stopped my construction but kept my armor. Before I knew it, I started to like him more and more. I pushed away the thought of "the one who kept me safe and protected me," and I began to date him. My therapist, grandmother, and aunts were concerned but talked about how happy I was. My walls began to be a defense against others, and he grew closer to me to be allowed inside the camp. Others who did not like him or had concerns became the enemy, and if he disapproved — because he was the one who was a self-built person and emotionally stable — I kicked them out of my tribe.

The efforts of "Mr. Bootstraps" were consistent with a few warning signs. I still had my weapons, and with each warning sign, I initiated the wall construction again and started to lock others out. Each woman that looked at him, the ones he danced with at fraternity parties, or even the ones he thought I never knew about, made me build a wall around him to keep out "the enemies." He had to be kept safe by me, so I brought him further into the camp. By the time I graduated with my bachelor's in biology, the wall of "defiance" was complete, and my camp became a camp of two... Now, I just needed to maintain my power and build my next wall carefully, as I was upset with myself for abandoning all my goals.

Once again, I was determined to live my life the way I wanted, with no one else making decisions for me. I was headed to nursing school to become a nurse practitioner to work in psychiatry. I needed more goals to work on and not to compromise at the expense of myself. However, I had the summer before nursing school to start working on a "power" wall. Let the construction begin.

Being in nursing school provided a certain level of freedom as I was away from where I lost friends, my voice, needed my walls, and amour. However, with this experience, I wanted to build myself to get back to who I was and feel powerful again. I felt protected to a point as me and "Mr. Bootstraps" were in two separate places, states and paths in our careers and life. Red flags were apparent but choosing to ignore them was easier to make the relationship work and feeling like he was "the one to protect me." He was my everything. I loved him with all my heart, but I was not willing to say no to being a nurse practitioner. I wanted more and needed more, but I was unsure how to ask him what I needed to feel like I could accomplish anything.

Nursing school was more challenging than college. However, my soulmate made me feel like I could do anything as he "pulled himself up by his bootstraps" while doing a great job of building a life for us with a great company. I felt powerful with him but powerless in nursing school. I was not the smart one anymore, and I was unsure how to deal with others who were just as intelligent and high achievers as me.

I felt intimidated by the stressors of being a minority from an HBCU, and I leaned on the one person in my camp. My parents and sisters were in the camp, but he was the one I trusted in, and he protected my emotions. Yet, again, enemies attempted to enter our camp, but I had my amour ready to fight them off until one day when I did not meet a need for him, and I realized that he was bringing others into my camp, and eventually he chose them. My camp was in ruins. The "power" wall I was building was now destroyed once again. My everything had betrayed me and ruined my camp. I felt violated, empty, and devastated to the point that I was so wounded and reinforced the walls "protection" and "defiance." I fought to get through my bachelor's in nursing after failing one course, not graduating with my original class, and started to study for the National Council Licensure Examination (NCLEX). However, the one thing any instructor will tell you about the NCLEX, or nursing boards, was that you could not be heartbroken, in grief, or under any type of stress to take this test. "Mr. Bootstraps" was not interested in speaking with me due to having "a supply" of women to occupy him at the time.

When I failed the NCLEX, I called him, and he did not even care. He said, "You left me for nursing school, so why should I care?" He had already taken his "new supply" to meet his family in a matter of three months! Man, my power was gone… I was alone and now knew that "Mr. Bootstraps" was no longer my soulmate, and one by one, over the next three months, I began reconstructing the walls I chose to knock down because of him. When I got over the hurt and the anger, the wall of "secrecy" was back up, and I started studying for the NCLEX in silence. I worked and studied and was alone in this journey… I wondered where my son was, wondered why life had seemed so hard since the rape and why I was not worthy of true love. For months I studied until I became Shana Smalls RN and started working in a local hospital on their transplant unit. I thought maybe now I could work on my wall of "power." Perhaps now I could get back to simply Shana and still be who I set out to be.

I waged one more battle with the nursing school and my health, which I let my wall of "secrecy" hid from my friends and family. I was not speaking to many of them anyway, but I had mastered the skill of being alone and in my own strength. Getting into the Master's program of nursing put me back on my path, and I would not allow cancer to take over. Once again, I was the minority student since I was only one of two in our program of five students. I was on a path of healing from losing my voice, friendships when I chose a man over them, and not knowing where my kid was. I wanted my voice back. I missed my friends, and I wanted my kid back.

I had met someone who "had a family structure and his act together." He was a breath of fresh air; he knew what he wanted, and I was it. He encouraged me to find my voice, but those walls were sensitive, and I was not willing to tear them down for him. As the months passed, "the one who had a family structure and his act together" got closer, and I really liked him, and he met my family. Anyone who knows me knows that if you met Granddolly, she was the one who approved if you could go to the next stage. She never really liked "Mr. Bootstraps" and was glad he was gone. Nearly two years had passed, and I did not hear from him until one day he called.

"Mr. Bootstraps" wanted back in, and, once again, the person who he'd brought to meet his family was now "crazy," and he had to let her go to get back to his soulmate. Who was he talking about? It could not have been me, right? At that time, I was with "had a family structure and his act together," and things were going well. However, I had not told him about the rape, my son, and my walls. I was building my "power" wall as I was getting ready to be a nurse practitioner since I was finishing my Master's. Of course, I loved and had a history with "Mr. Bootstraps," but it was different. I was not sure if he was truly the one for me. I felt like my life was my own, and I had accomplished so much without him. I felt free and peaceful with "had a family structure and his act together." Then, one day I got an unexpected call that would rock my whole camp and cause me to drop my armor.

A woman named Anna wanted to know if I had a son by the name of Shane Michael. How did she know his name? How had she found me? Nothing else at that moment mattered, and I told her it would be a pleasure to meet him. I drove two hours to meet "mini-me." It took me back to that moment in October 1998 when we met, and he knew me the minute he walked around the corner. We were both nervous, excited, and sad. We were excited to meet, and my armor fell off. I put down my sword and opened the camp. "Mr. Bootstraps" pressed harder despite my advances and then showed up at my Master's graduation ceremony. And I felt like all my power was gone again, and I surrendered it for our familiar history. I gave up "had a family structure and his act together" for a person whom I was not sure if he really loved me with all of him like I did since he was a part of my camp again… Of course, now his life was not in S.C. but in N.C., which would take me away from my entire family. But he wanted only the best for me, to be my protector, and I settled for just that although I wanted more… Let the adventure to losing myself begin.

I took the test to become a nurse practitioner and failed by one point. He thought that I needed a trip to N.C., even though I was still living in S.C. I loved who I was working with, being near my cousins, and taking the path to work with a residency program. He surprisingly proposed to me on this trip, and I said yes despite being disappointed that my family was not there with us. His church family, who were very nice strangers to me, were so excited at the sight of this beautiful couple becoming one. I started planning a wedding, even though I never felt more alone in my camp.

The wedding planning began in S.C., but he thought it would be too expensive and decided to move it to N.C. My family tradition of getting married at Old Bethel United Methodist Church had been broken. Everyone in my family would come to S.C. to get married, we all got together to plan the bridal shower, and we all went to pick out a dream dress. I did none of these things. I went to David's Bridal with a gracious church member and picked out my dress this way. I picked the second dress I tried on and bought it that day. My mother, my sister, or his sisters were not there. For once, I did not see "the fantastic four" anywhere in my camp.

I also knew that I took the experience of celebrating love away from them, which felt like I was just settling and not expressing myself and my needs for our wedding. My money paid for our wedding while he gave his opinions, including me moving to N.C. the year of the wedding. I commuted for at least one hour and worked the night shift. The wedding I dreamed of was gone, and it was all my fault. My walls were intact, but the protection was gone, my armor was breaking, and I wanted them back. The closer the wedding got, the more lost I felt, and I wanted someone to stop me. I felt so lost, and he had no idea. I kept hoping it would get better. My tribe was not a part of my big day, my line sister, my day ones from Alice drive middle and Sumter High, but I did have my fifth grade best friend there but not at my side.

The day had finally arrived where I would walk down the aisle, but no one was still listening to what I wanted. The music was not the songs I wanted; the sit-down dinner was good, but still, it was not the dream reception I'd imagined. The whole morning felt wrong. When my dad came in, he read my face and reminded me that you should feel peaceful and like this person is a part of your team when you marry someone. "You can build with this person, and on your toughest days, he will have your back, and you will have his." I cried and told him that everyone was here, and this man loves me and will make sure I get my camp back in order. He will help me with my armor. Yet, I did not feel like he could, and I was shaking all the way down the aisle, but I was determined to be happy with "Mr. Bootstraps," who would have his own business one day. One day, he would be a wonderful father to Shane and our other children, and we were going to build a wonderful life together. I would be the submissive wife who takes care of my husband, prays for him, and protects her household. I was going to be an overachiever. Yet, we were not prepared for the biggest challenge that would devastate me not long after.

My diva of an aunt was not doing well, living with pancreatic cancer. She had surgery, but the cancer had spread to the point that she had to stop her chemotherapy. This all occurred the first year of our marriage, although her battle had been ongoing since nursing school. I won my battle, and I knew she was stronger than me, yet a big part of me knew I was losing her. I also later found out my grandmother was experiencing the same cancer, but she seemed fine. My husband was supportive and accompanied me to see my aunt one weekend. I spoke to her about my struggles with my new husband... how I should dress for church, what friends to hang out with, what bills to pay, amongst other things. However, I was the submissive wife, and I allowed my husband to take the lead, no matter how controlling it felt. She told me to communicate my feelings with him, but I never said a word. I spent the whole weekend with her, and she warned me she would not be back when I returned. She made me promise to protect my heart and watch how vulnerable I was with him.

She died later that day, and I spoke of her strength at her funeral. I decided that my walls were going back up on that day, my armor was going back on, and my camp, who was my essential crew, was coming back in. I need to get back to me now! Yet, less than a month later, my grandmother declined and died as well. Unfortunately, my husband could not attend and what he did not realize is that I had lost two out of three most important people who were holding my wall of "secrecy." My mother and father held my wall of "protection," and my sister held the wall of "defiance" with me. It was now time to attain my power to get through the biggest loss of my life in 2009 that my husband could not understand.

I held myself together as we continued to build our marriage. I hung out with the approved friends instead of being with mine. I needed to be with my friends to deal with the loss, yet I had no power, and the voice that I had left was dying, despite having so many blessings happening. We bought our first house. I passed the nurse practitioner boards and started my first NP job. However, I was not happy. I held onto my armor and my walls until one day, he crashed through my wall of "secrecy." Shane was in his junior year and took prom pictures, and my husband posted them on Facebook and Instagram. My secret was out, and I had to finally tell my family what had happened to me back in 1998. I had to say to my friends, including my day ones, who I kept silent about. It was disrespectful and triggering. The nightmares started again, and having sexual relations with my husband became difficult. Little did I know, my wall of "secrecy" was destroyed due to stressors felt by my husband. I wanted to continue to build it, but it was much harder, and I felt like I owed him as he had stood by me (in his own way). I turned to friends to assist me in maintaining my marriage and keeping me objective since we had issues connecting. I would find out that others connected with him despite how hard I worked to make things work between us.

We decided that we were ready to grow our family, and we started working on it, but I had some issues (due to previous cancer issues) until we were finally blessed with Christopher John aka "The Kingdom Kid." I finally felt like I could drop my walls and show my sons how strong of a woman their mother was and that she does have a voice. When I held that small human being in my arms, who also knew me, smiled at me, and held my hand… I realized that I had no idea who I had become. What had happened to me? And why was I getting phone calls from random women?

"Mr. Bootstraps", my husband, had once again had others a part of my camp, and my walls made it possible. He had an exercise group where many women joined and started talking to him more than me. It did not matter how much I encouraged him, provided funding for his desires; they had a hold on his ego, and me guarding my walls and not my marriage sheltered me from the obvious. My husband did not love me for me, no matter how many things I paid for, working more hours, or trying to fix things. Now, I needed to get my family to stop guarding my walls, allow the remaining three walls to come crashing down. I had to fight with my armor only for the following: my voice, my light, and to find my identity.

I had to start over; I had to go back to my roots. However, going to my roots led to my husband accusing me of cheating with no proof, me finding out that the savings in the bank was gone, and my sexual issues, along with other issues were being discussed with co-workers, exercise group members, and anyone else who would listen. He felt like a single parent while I worked to pay for daycare and the majority of our bills. Yet, I was in therapy trying to fix things to make him happy. In the meantime, I still wanted to build with him to meet his desires, but I was not sure how and I wanted to be held accountable and understand his perspective.

I learned that he had been flirting with others, and they felt like I was in the way. I knew that starting over might mean that I had to move away from him to fully build myself if he could not clear up or validate any issues with me. I had to start from the beginning, and I asked him about so many of our issues, and he became defensive and vague. I ended up asking for a separation, which devastated him, me, and our family. No matter how I looked at the situation, I needed to put Shana first finally. With my walls down and my family standing behind me, I was at the most vulnerable stage of my life, but I also felt the freest. I thought he would "see me," understand what I meant to him, and come back and explain... We eventually moved forward with the terms of our separation. I paid for spousal support, income taxes, everything needed by our sons, but the further we moved apart, the more he interacted with other women, so I decided to pursue divorce.

I remained by myself, allowing many good things to happen... I struggled to find my identity, stay strong for the boys, who were confused but resilient until a light came on. Our divorce was finalized, yet I wasn't exactly free as ten days later, "Mr. Bootstraps" had a heart attack, and I was needed again by his side. I was his first call. One of the nurses, who knew me, told me that he had no heartbeat, and they would continue to work on him. When I arrived at the hospital, they were taking him to the lab. He looked gray and could barely talk. As I sat and waited, all I could think about was the last few months and how he was someone I did not know anymore. I wanted him to live so that we could start over, but the wait was so long, and I was getting worried. The reality of the situation began hitting me as the text messages, and phone calls from the other women started. Each one meaner than the next, who knew more about me than I did about them.

The doctor came out and told me that he was alive, but they were not sure for how long. His family was on the way, and yet I felt like my life had paused. He was alive, and everyone rallied around him and gave me looks, yet he said, "Don't believe the background noise. I want us." Yet, I clutched my sword harder. According to the doctors, he could not be alone. It was decided that he would come to my house while keeping his apartment. "The one who pulled himself up by his bootstraps" now became "Mr. I came back different." We had a lot to talk about. He wanted a blank slate, but too much had happened. Thirty thousand dollars were gone, the exercise group was not given boundaries, and as a wife, I'd been disrespected. As a wife, I needed to know where things went wrong, could we make it right, and how could we do it together? Can we build, and did he understand why I worked the three jobs as a nurse practitioner? Why was the savings gone, and why did I not know anything about it? How did I fall for his charming ways only to meet a whole other person?

"Mr. I came back different" just revised his approach. "Mr. Bootstraps" remained intact, and I felt like all the walls I'd knocked down for him, I needed to rebuild. I needed to prepare the bricks. However, my tribe, who had assisted me in building an open, free, and peaceful camp, reminded me of my armor, and I had protected me and not them. I don't need the walls as I can protect, live in my truth and not secrecy, be open to new things and not fight everything. Now, I can tap into my power authentically. "Mr. I came back different" was no longer my happily ever after and was not my Superman, Aquaman, Clark Kent, or Bruce Wayne.

This Wonder Woman had found herself through the separation, divorce, giving away $70,000, and his heart attack! I was ready to take on the world. She realized how beautiful, fierce, flawless, and powerful she is! For so long, she had been carrying everyone and their issues and not speaking up for herself. Although he was back, and he was different, she had evolved. Did he see her? Was he ready for the evolved version of her? Would he be ready for the questions I had? In reality, he wasn't and left again. It was OK, and I felt so peaceful. So, now it was time for Shana to be selfish and put herself first. It was time for Shana to walk in her truth and see the twenty-year relationship for what it was… History and not being a priority but an option, and I accepted the option status. This Wonder Woman was tired of feeling guilty for ultimately doing what was best for her child, tired of carrying baggage and walking through the dark tunnel of life. I had to forgive myself and let go! Letting go of control, responding instead of reacting, and embracing healing allowed me to drop the walls I thought I needed. I was already protected, living in my truth, and now I was finally open to embrace "the lifelong lover" that came looking for me. "Mr. Bootstraps" moved on, and so did I. My space has been full of happiness, peace, and love. He is no longer a factor of hurt or disappointment but one of thanks and blessings. He was a journey I needed to experience to get greater!

My story is not unique, but it is mine. However, you are never alone and do not need to start suffering in silence. Living in your truth is so vital. You have to embrace your struggle and sit in your emotions. Giving up my child was devastating, but I had to process it in therapy for a long time. I had to be held accountable and be unapologetically me no matter who did not understand my intentions.. I had to feel it and walk through it. My relationship, marriage, and divorce were devastating and so heartbreaking. Yet, I felt so guilty. Forgiveness is vital for yourself first and for others to free your heart, mind, and soul. Yes, forgiveness is key, and you need to spend time alone with yourself. Hurt people, hurt others. Watch your interactions while you are healing. Moving forward is one thing, but you will not be opened to receiving the right kind of love until it finds you.

Acknowledgements

To my parents, Tyrone and Kathleen… Thank you for all of your love, support, encouragement to be authentically me. I can never thank you enough for everything I am, who you taught me to be and, to love and forgive everyone no matter what!

To my one and only sister, Shari… We been rocking hard since 1985 and you continue to inspire and remind me to be unapologetically me!! No words can express how much I love you!!

To my best friends Sean and Isaiah… thank you for all your "old man" and "Superman" wisdom and you reminding me to never stop going after all I deserve.

To Dawn, Jennifer, Teshia and Veronica thank you for your unconditional friendship and true sisterhood that has stood the test of time.. I love yall!!!

To my truest tribe members thank you for embracing me and allowing me to sow into your lives…

To the man who helped me believe in love, peace and effortless happiness; I love and honor you forever… Thank you for finding me when I needed you!!! #fullcircle #everyday

Dedication

To the women and men who struggle everyday to know your worth…
Who feel like no one understands you, who feel like you cannot move
forward… I want this chapter to touch you in a way that you understand
your worth, demand it and walk in it. Stand in your truth and forgive
those who hurt you. Healing is so necessary!!!

Reflections

_____

_____

_____

_____

_____

_____

_____

_____

_____

_____

_____

_____

_____

_____

_____

_____

_____

_____

_____

_____

_____

Reflections

Reflections

Proof

www.ingramcontent.com/pod-product-compliance
Lightning Source LLC
Chambersburg PA
CBHW050407030726
47503CB00006B/2069